I0681283

Willesden Herald

New Short Stories 1

Pretend Genius Press

London, New York, San Francisco, Seattle, Washington D.C.

www.pretendgenius.com

Published simultaneously in the United States and Great Britain in 2007
by Pretend Genius Press
London, New York, San Francisco, Seattle, Washington D.C.

This compilation copyright © The Willesden Herald 2007
Edited by Stephen Moran

ISBN 978-0-9778526-2-8

Acknowledgements

Gosh, I have nothing prepared! Many thanks to Mikey Delgado for help with the selections, to Zadie Smith for judging in the international Willesden Herald short story competition, to Stratos Fountoulis for the cover design, to Sarah Crown and all at Guardian Books for their support. Thanks to everyone at the Willesden Herald and Pretend Genius Press for their belief in the imaginary. Most of all, thanks to writers who continue the great tradition of the short story, as you are about to see.

Stephen Moran
Willesden, 2007

Contents

Contents

Willie Davis

Kid in a Well

I never work on days when there's a fire in town. It's a holiday as far as I'm concerned, and not just because it means the end of the world to some poor bastard, or family thereof. I do sympathize, but a fire's bigger than that. Not all fires, of course. People burning brush doesn't do much for me. It's a controlled burn—all the smoke is gray—and I can work through that. But accidental fires, with black, oak-smelling smoke, ought to stop a town cold. For one, it's a beacon a whole city can see and smell, and so it's on everyone's minds, whether they're talking about it or not. Behind every little head nod, and gruff how's-it-going, you are and whoever you're talking to is thinking, What's it take for that to happen to me? The wind blows south instead of southeast, or a fleck of canola oil jumps from the frying pan to the drapes, and that's me out of my home, begging mercy from my friends and neighbors. A city as small as Hazard, Kentucky can't have a home catch fire without everyone knowing how close we came to losing whatever walls we have. So on the days of a house fire, I don't work in celebration of all of us who're spared. Then again, I don't work too much anyway, so another day away shouldn't cripple the economy.

As it happened, I was in the dry cleaners, our family business, getting alternate earfuls from my two baby brother bosses when I caught a glimpse of black smoke rising from the mountains. I'd love to say I smelled it first, or sixth-sensed it, or something along those lines, but that's not true. I just got a lucky look and then snuck out the back door, away from clean clothes for the rest of the day.

The fire was high on the mountain where everyone could see it—the best kind. When that happens, people keep their heads angled up in the air, so they drift slightly when they walk. The only folks who look normal are the old timers who never do anything, but sit on their porch and stare up at the sky all day anyway. I never liked those sorts of old people, men and women alike. Maybe that's heresy, but it seems like after a certain age, people's minds and goodwill shrivel up with their bodies. What passes for wisdom is really just the stripped down bones of their thoughts, the catchphrases they can remember now that the rest of the story's gone. I know I'm more old than young, and if I can make it another ten years with my liver unexploded, the odds are better than even I'll wind up just like them, but I still say there's something unnatural about decrepit people staring out at the world like it's got something to prove.

The streets were mostly empty, so I made it down to Holiday's Bar, my old hangout back when I could drink like an adult. I like the afternoon people in bars, or, at least, I like them in the afternoon. By nighttime, most of them would turn either blubbery or snarling, but so long as the sun was out, they always wanted to talk. Anyway, it was healthy to spend time in bars, with old, drunk friends, no matter what those perky, straight-toothed counselors say. They'd rather have it build up in your mind like an old girlfriend or a boogeyman in your closet, so that you can't go to sleep without nightmaring over it. I'd rather have it in front of me where I can see it as it is; just flat, brown liquid in a cup.

Don Holiday, the owner, stood behind the bar, with his belly dangling over his belt, wiping the insides of empty glasses with a Kentucky Wildcat dishrag. "Good God, it's Frankie Clay," he said when he saw me. "I swear you spend more time in here now than you did when you's drinking." He only knows three jokes, and this is one of them. "Cup of coffee?"

"Orange pop." I sidled up to the bar, and tried to rub away the pain in my lower spine. At first, I thought the bar was empty, but after a second look, I saw there were the same number of liquid-lunchers as always, but they weren't scattered out like normal. Instead, they were clustered in the corner watching the TV. "What's this?" I said to Don, when he brought me my drink. "The Reds playing?"

"Nah" he said. "There's a boy in Oklahoma who got hisself stuck in a well. They been trying to rescue him for a few hours now."

"That's it?" I took a sip of pop and gargled it in the back of my throat. "Why don't they just yank him out?" I turned to face the crowd. "Why's this on TV anyway? Is he an ambassador's kid or something?"

"He's not a fish, Frankie." Don slapped me with his dishrag. "You can't just drop a line and bring him up. His back may be broke, and if they don't do it proper, then he could wind up a cripple. Say Alex," he called over to the group in the corner. "What're they saying about this kid?"

Gray-faced Alex Hobbs turned around and yelled, "They got his voice coming up out the top. They say he's okay, but no one knows for certain. Maybe he hit his head, they say. No one knows right now."

"Great." I swirled the orange pop in the back of my throat. I used to drink whiskey this same way, and it was better. "I'd hate to learn this kid's got brain damage. It's not like he's smart enough to keep out of wells in the first place."

Everyone groaned. I still couldn't make out all the people, but my eyes were adjusting to the dark, and I was hoping I could pick them out by their voices when they yelled at me.

"Come on, now." This was Pops Larkin, my old boss from back in the days when I could still get semigainful employment from people who didn't share my last name. He was a small, but powerful man, and he spoke with a thick croak that sounded like a flat trombone. "He's a kid. A poor boy who didn't know any better. You telling me you don't care if this kid makes it or not?"

"No one's saying that." I took another sip of orange pop, but could barely taste it. "But it's just one kid. In Oklahoma, some place I've never been, and no one here's ever been. I'm rooting for him, sure, but if he doesn't make it then so what? You guys know my brother, Arnold, and his wife? She got cancer about a year ago. Got her left tit chopped off. That's the same as some kid in a hole out west. They're both sad."

"For one, it was three years ago," Pops said. "Don't try to get our sympathy with it if you can't remember when it was." He walked up close to me, and threw a wadded up bill on the bar. "One more, Donnie." He turned to me. "What's your point, anyway? What's your brother's wife got to do with anything?"

"All right, fine." I drained the last of my drink, and crunched an ice cube with my back teeth. "You boys remember that Baby Jessica they got from the well? I saw a picture of her when she was maybe, like, sixteen. Braces and pimples and big and fat. I was thinking, Put her back, please."

"Frankie, take it easy, man." Don snatched up Pops' money, and put an Amber beer on the bar. "It's not like there's two sides here. A kid's in a well, and we all want him out. What you trying to start a fight for?"

"Starting nothing," I said. "But there are two sides. There's the side that wants to watch live video of a top of a well, and there's the side that says maybe something better's on. Something that'll give us a little more conversation, at least. Baseball's on, I know, even if the Reds aren't. Anybody else want to change the channel? Am I alone on this? Come on, a show of hands."

"It's on every station," Don said. "Anyway, it's my bar, and we watch what I say."

"Every station," I said. "Christ alive, every single station's got some redneck sheriff staring down a hole in the ground? This isn't real. Has anyone even noticed there's a house on fire just up the mountain? That's not Oklahoma either. That's here."

"So what?" Don said. "So you think we should go up and look at that instead? That's better than this?"

"Come on, Buddy, don't you have kids?" This was Alex Hobbs again. He'd known me for years, but kept drunk enough to where he could ask the same question over and over and stay surprised at the answer. "You know what it's like when a child's in trouble."

"I like kids," I said. "It's sad when of them gets killed or cancer. But this is different. Kid's probably liking it down there. Just get to stare up at the sky like it's a big blue television. It's relaxing. Plus, he's got all the attention he wants. Probably'll wind up meeting the governor. Maybe some prick's going to write a folk song about him. All things being equal, diving down the well's not a bad business move for this boy."

"Here," Don said. He poured a rail whiskey straight up, and plopped it in front of me. "Go on, take it. When you was drinking, you were better at pretending to not be such an asshole. Go on, I won't charge you."

I stared up at him. Just like every drunk's got to get used to those folks who talk to him like a foreigner or child, every recovering drunk's got to get used to people thinking he's going to go into spasms at the sight or smell of the first free drink. "I'm not drinking it, Donnie. You know that."

"Calm down," he said. "I'm just kidding."

I heard the door swing open, and I turned around. Jesse Dunaway—a college kid, working at the dry cleaners for the summer—stuck his head in and smiled when he saw me. When he was in high school, I used to watch him playing small forward for the Hazard Bulldogs. I remember he had the best pump fake I'd ever seen, and, even now, nursing a drinking problem and smoking like a diesel, he kept something of that athlete's grace about him. "Jesse, my boy," I said. "Come on in. I just bought you a drink."

"No thanks," he said. "I'm on the clock right now."

"I know," I said. "My brother sent you to come here and collect me, right?"

He nodded. "He saw you were gone, so he figured

you came here."

I patted the stool next to mine. "Come on, I'm your boss, and I'm telling you to have a drink. Sit."

He walked over to me gingerly, and sat down. When I slid the whiskey in front of him, he narrowed his eyes, and looked between me and Don. "You buy this?"

"Yeah, I bought it for you, now drink it. It's full. I didn't steal any."

"He didn't drink it," Don said. "All he's had is orange soda, so don't worry."

Jesse looked down at his hands and flashed a nervous smile. He took a small sip of his drink and looked over at the crowd in front of the television. "The Reds playing?"

"Two peas in a pod, you two." Don cracked a sideways smirk. "No, some of us were concerned about this kid in Oklahoma stuck in a well. Frankie's about to tell us how kids are meant for drowning, and every well should have a baby or two in it. We're all listening."

I turned around. They were all listening. When Christ grants me an audience, I usually don't hesitate to exploit His goodwill, but I needed to clear the air first. I leaned in close to Jesse and blew a breath on him. "Smell that?" I said. "No booze on it. Don't go telling my brothers I'm drinking. Not even that you suspect it, if you do."

He shrugged, smiled, and leaned back, away from me. "I don't suspect anything." He took a slow drink of whiskey and set it down on the bar. "Maybe I'm the only one, but I don't."

"Good boy." I turned around. The crowd—at least what passes for a crowd—was still more interested in me than the television, but I knew that wouldn't last forever. "Tell me, Jesse." I spoke loud enough for everyone to hear me. "You heard anything about this case on TV we're talking about?"

"A couple guys at the cleaners were talking about it." He sniffed his whiskey, and held it in front of his face, but didn't drink. "What're you going to do?"

On TV, they showed a still picture of a smiling, curly-headed boy in overalls. Pale skin, very dark hair, and almost Italian eyes. Without realizing it, I assumed he'd be a blonde.

"They shouldn't do that," Jesse said. "Showing his picture, I mean." He reached over the bar, grabbed a fingerful of ice, and dropped it in his drink. "I know they got to show something, but now everyone's going to think he looks like that. When they bring him out, and he's bleeding and purple, we're all going to be horrified. It's like a card trick the news plays. Draw you in expecting one thing and then show something else."

"You know, I once saved a black kid from drowning," I said. "This was down in Florida when I was a kid."

"You did not," Pops said. "Stop lying."

"No one's lying," I said. "A little black kid, maybe six years old. If I hadn't have been there, there's no way he'd have made it."

"Seriously?" Jesse said. He lit a cigarette and laid the pack on the bar. "This isn't a joke or anything, is it? Like, you didn't try to drown the kid and then change your mind at the last second?"

Don slid me over a fresh glass of orange pop. For the first time, I saw he was sweating—not much, but a visible sheen that ran from the bags under his eyes to his moustache. This wasn't just the fat man's sweat we all have to deal with in July. He looked sick.

"When I was seventeen, my dad was thinking of franchising the cleaners. There was a place in Tampa he thought he could take over, and so the family made a vacation of it. Now, at the time—seventeen, remember—I was working on this moustache. I was growing it thin like the Mexicans wear them, but it wasn't coming in right."

"Well, stop the presses, Frankie," Pops said. He laughed and slapped the table. "'Fat Alcoholic Once Attempted Moustache.'"

"Seriously, buddy." This came from some shaggy, baby-faced blonde under the television. I didn't recognize him, but if I had to guess, I'd say he was a distant relation to Pops. "Get to the drowning."

I stood up. If I was getting asked questions by strangers, then I figured it was all right to take command of the room. "Ingrates, every one of you. Do you go to church and say, 'Get to the crucifixion?' I'm setting a scene here. Trying to make you bums understand what's going on." I spun around toward Jesse. "Now, where was I?"

"Moustache," he said. "You're growing it Spanish style, but it wasn't coming in real well."

"Right," I said. "That actually didn't have much to do with the story. But remember, we're on vacation, and Dad's working most of the time. So my brothers are about nine and eight, and they want to go to the zoo and watch the lions get fed, and throw peanuts at elephants, and shit like that. I'm happy to play along, but no self-respecting seventeen year-old wants to spend his Florida trip looking at a white rhino."

"You were self-respecting at seventeen?" said Pops. "What happened?"

"So I'm packed up and ready to go to the zoo, and I

see this Asian girl from out the window. Looks like a pin-up, this girl does, and she's lying by the pool, getting sun. I'd never seen a TV-star looking woman before. I was like you guys, settling for thinking about the tan-in-a-bottle Hazard cheerleaders, but once I see this Asian, I couldn't think of much else."

"What's wrong with Hazard cheerleaders?" the baby-faced blonde in the corner said. "My sister cheers for Hazard."

"Well, congratulations," I told him. "I don't know you, but I'm looking at you now, and trust me, unless she's adopted, your sister can't hold a candle to this Asian girl."

"Hey," the man said. He stood up, but I knew he wasn't going anywhere. I was too old and too soft for this guy to get any pleasure from smacking me around. It would've been an ugly scene—a vicious, one-sided pounding that wouldn't have played well in his memory.

Then Pops stood up and put up a pacifying hand. "He didn't say nothing's wrong with Hazard cheerleaders, he said he used to think about them, and if you're wondering what's his fucking point, you're not alone. You're growing a Spanish moustache, staring at a slope, and about to save a black boy. When you were drinking, you could at least tell us lies without making yourself into a league of nations. What's your point?"

"My point?" I rapped my knuckles on the bar. "Jesse, tell them my point."

He shrugged. "His point is that I don't know what his point is, because he's not done with his story, because you guys keep interrupting."

"Give that man a refill," I said. "He knows what I'm talking about." I took a step in the direction of the crowd in the corner. "Now, let's see, I was talking about the Asian. You get the picture, right? So once I see her, I know what I got to do. I tell my mom I got a stomach virus, so I can stay in the hotel all day. I was too shy to talk to her, but I wanted to keep looking at her. So I wait until they're gone, pour some of my dad's rum in a Styrofoam cup. I knew I couldn't just sit next to her and make googly eyes without getting maced, so I look for a book or something I can pretend to read. But nobody in my family reads, so there were no books in the room, except for my brother's Encyclopedia Browns and that might give off the wrong impression."

"Oh yeah," Jesse said. "You wouldn't want her to think the seventeen year-old who spends his vacation ogling her was unsophisticated."

"Right," I said. "So I go in and take out the Gideon's Bible. My mom left her compact in the sink, so I taped it on the inside pages. That way, I could admire my new moustache without seeming vain in front of the Asian."

"You taped a mirror to the Bible?" Don said.

On T.V., a cartoon sun hawking detergent or floor wax danced on some blonde family's supper table, which was good news. If they cut to commercial, that meant they were still a long ways away from fishing the kid out. If they rescued him in mid-story, then I'd never get the crowd back. "So, I'm poolside, sitting in one of those white plastic chairs, having a time, staring at the Asian and myself, trying to figure out who's prettier. Then, from out of nowhere—"

"From out of nowhere," Pops said. He laughed and clapped his hands until the sound disappeared into his smoker's cough. "I love how he builds it up. Let me guess. Then, *from out of nowhere*, our conquering sack of guts, Frankie Clay, sees this black boy underwater. He puts on his cape with the big S on it, saves the boy, gives him mouth to mouth, marries his Oriental, then goes on to drink his life away. Is that it?"

"Then, from out of nowhere," I said. "This geriatric, old man comes racing in to ruin the story. But as our narrator is a righteous man, he will not be dissuaded by feeble naysayers. As I was saying, then, from the pool, I see this black kid paddling around in the shallow end. Cute as a fucking June bug, this kid was. Big afro hair, Bermuda shorts, those plastic things kids put on their arms."

"Floaties," Jesse said. "That's how I learned to swim."

"Yeah, Floaties," I said. "I mean, this kid could've been a Huxtable."

"Sounds like you fell in love twice that day," Pops said.

"Rim shot, please," I said. "My God, Pops, looking like Don Rickles don't make you funny." I walked back to the bar, and grabbed my orange pop. "No, I didn't fall in love at all that day, even if I wish I did. I just thought it's worth mentioning that I noticed the kid whose life I'm about to save. It's called foreshadowing." I took a swig of pop, and then sucked the flavor off the back of my lips. "Like I was saying, the kid was cute, but the Asian was massage parlor beautiful. Guess which one I'd rather look at?"

"The Asian?" Alex Hobbs asked. "I mean, if it was me, that's who I'd look at."

"Yes Alex, that's right," I said. "I went back to looking at the Asian. But I'm only eyeing her for maybe a minute and a half when I hear this couple going at it on the other side of the pool."

"Going at it?" Jesse said. "You mean, fighting, or making out?"

"Fighting." I walked back to the center of the crowd. "This black couple, the kid's parents, I think. The guy looks rough, like he used to be handsome, but bloated up. Had red eyes like a junkie, and he kept saying 'weak.' 'This is *weak*, man. This whole trip is *weak*.' His wife, this little fat chunk of a woman, just stood there and took it. Sometimes, she rolled her head, but that's it. It was pretty dull as far as fights go, but I kept an eye on them, hoping it might escalate."

"What were they arguing over?" Don said.

"I don't know. The guy said he was getting a can of Coke, and the girl says, 'Well, get me something too.' He says, 'That's weak' and stomps off without her. About this time, I decide I'm no longer interested, and I wanted to see what my moustache looks like when I'm no longer interested. Except I see the kid's still in the pool. And he's heading for the deep end."

"But he's got the floaties on," Jesse said. He lit another cigarette and French inhaled, which surprised me. I knew ex-athletes could smoke, but I didn't actually think they'd be good at it. "You can't sink with those. Even if his head goes under, he's not really in trouble."

"That's what I thought," I said. "So the first time he dips underwater, I'm not really worried. But then he doesn't come up. I stand up and go over to the edge. I say, 'Hey Sailor'—this is true, I called him sailor—I say, 'Hey Sailor, you okay down there? You need a hand or something?'"

"What'd he say?" Alex Hobbs asked.

"He said, 'Ten-Four buddy, I'm doing just fine. By the way, I love your moustache.'"

"'Ten-Four?'" Alex said. "Like a trucker, he

talked?"

"No he didn't say that." I downed half of my pop and gurgled it in the back of my throat. "He was underwater. What's he going to say?"

"But he still had the floaties on," Jesse said. "I mean, worse comes to worst, he's still floating. You just got to turn him around, right?"

"Well, I couldn't see him," I said. "So I went up to the edge of the pool and look down. The kid's kicking like a mule, spinning around in circles. At this point, I realize this is all he's been taught about swimming, that he's got to kick. I shout down at him, 'Use your arms, buddy, like this,' and try to act out a doggie paddle, but he can't hear me. Now, I know he's underwater, and I know he's in trouble, but he's still got the plastic on his arms, so I still think he'll be fine. Then, all the sudden, I get this clear-eyed vision, and I know this kid's going to drown if I don't stop it. I saw that black kid drowned, with that pale loose skin the drowning corpses have, and those water red eyes, and I saw me beating on his chest, and him trying to spit that water up out at me, but it never getting past his throat. I saw all that, maybe not like it was a hundred percent real, but at least as clear as I could see that Asian's tits, and I had to stop it. So, I sat down and took off my sneakers."

"You took off your sneakers?" Pops said. "The boy's drowning, you got religion wanting to save this kid so bad, and you stop to take off your shoes? Why didn't you put zinc on your nose while you're at it?"

"What're you doing wearing sneakers at a pool, anyway?" Alex asked. "Didn't you have no flip flops?"

I snuck a glance at Jesse to see how he was taking it. He was acting distant, like he could hide from the story behind his cigarette smokescreen. It was an act, of course. He's not the sort that can remove himself from someone else's story. But the fact that he could be aware of himself enough to try to put on an act meant I wasn't telling it as well as I should. This story was easier to tell with a drink in your hand, but times change, and I ought to get used to telling it with orange pop and rotted teeth, instead of rye whiskey and a warm heart. "So I take off my sneakers—which, I agree, in retrospect, was a mistake—and dive in headfirst."

"Headfirst?" Jesse said.

"I know," I said. "Bad idea. Turns out the water wasn't as deep as I thought it'd be. I smack my forehead on the pool bottom, bleeding everywhere, and can't see a thing. To make it worse, I start flailing all my limbs around, trying to get up to the surface, and I kick the kid square in the stomach. Finally, I take my head out of the water, and it hurts to breathe, my lungs are so wet, but I calm myself, and get some air back. It's hot out there, and I remember not wanting to go back underwater. Except that kid's doing worse, much worse now that I kicked him, and I'd hate for people to think I dove in the pool to kick a drowning black boy. There's nothing worse than that."

"You could've shot him," Alex Hobbs said. "That'd have been worse. Molesting him would've been worse too."

"You're right, Alex," I said. "Still—although Alex raises a good point—I didn't want to kick a drowning boy. So I wipe the blood off my face, and go back under. I can't see all that well, but I make out this big brown blob, and scoop it out. We're both gasping for air, and I'm trying to take him to the shallow end, but it's all I can do to stand and carry the kid at the same time. Still, we make it over to the side, and for a while, it's just the two of us, panting, laying out on the concrete like a couple of beached whales. Neither of us is talking for a while, but then I realize I should ask his name. Before I can get to it, I hear this woman saying, 'What's all this.' It was the kid's mother, standing over me, out for blood. I can't really talk at first, I'm too tired, so I just gesture over at her son. 'I asked you a question,' she says, and she's shaking her head, making all her chin fat wobble from side to side like a turkey. 'Your son,' I said. 'He was in the water.' She says, 'I know he was in the water, motherfucker. I put him in the water.' I try sitting up, but I can't quite do it. She yanks the kid by the hand and waddles off."

I sat down in my original seat, and finished off my orange pop. They were looking at me, waiting for me to finish.

"So that's it?" Don said. "She just walked off?"

"Yes, that's it." I tried laughing, but it didn't sound real. "I saved the kid, what do you want me to do? Give a hundred dollars to the Red Cross in his name?"

"But you didn't really save him?" Don said. He emptied Jesse's ashtray and replaced it with a clean one. "The kid had his face in the water. You bellyflop on top of him, and get bawled out by his mom. That's not really saving a kid from drowning."

"Yeah it is," Jesse said. "No matter how he did it, if he doesn't jump in, the kid sinks. That's saving him, right?" He leaned closer to me. "What'd the Asian think?"

"Worst part about it," I said. "She'd fallen asleep, and missed the whole thing. The one heroic act of my life, and it didn't get me laid."

"I'm telling you, Frankie, it's not heroic," Don said. He poured himself a whiskey glass full of pale ale. "He wasn't drowning; he just had his head down. Ask his mom if it's heroic."

"It's not heroic," Pops said. "It's not heroic because it never happened."

"Exactly," the shaggy blonde said. "I was wondering how long we'd have to listen to this shit before someone called him on it."

Pops stood up and cocked his head back. "First of all, when was it? When you were a teenager, how likely was it that blacks and whites would share a swimming pool in Florida? Plus, the kid's got a flotation device, but he sinks anyway."

"He wasn't sinking," Don said. "He just had his head down."

"He wasn't sinking, because he didn't exist," Pops said. "Unless you believe that the Asian, wide awake one minute, falls asleep and stays asleep through a messy rescue, and a screaming match."

Jesse lit another cigarette. "I believe him." He coughed, and then started again. "I mean, what're we talking about? Sixties, early seventies? Florida's not Alabama—blacks and whites can share a hotel pool. Especially in a city like Tampa. As for the Asian, maybe she didn't exist, but I bet the black kid part is true."

Don topped off Jesse's whiskey, and leaned into him, conspiratorially. "You been gone a long time, kid. You didn't know this guy in his prime. He once told me he was Henry Clay's great grandson, so I'd pour him a free drink."

"Great *great* grandson," I said. "And why else would we have the same last name?"

"You see?" Don said. "You see what we have to deal with? Good God, this isn't even talking about the women. You know Molly Donaldson? He told her he was a Notary Public and a licensed massage therapist just to get her to have a drink with him. But he got her too drunk, and they both passed out on the bench over there."

"Wait a second," I said. "First, I didn't get too drunk—that was my plan to pass out next to her. Second, you're supposed to lie to women. If you count lying on dates, then every man in here's a liar ten times over."

"That wasn't a date," Pops said. "You just got her drunk."

"All right then," I said, "but if that's not a date, then I've never been on a date in my life."

"Can we back up a second?" Don said. He took a sip of some clear liquor he'd poured while we weren't looking. "At one point, this was about Frankie's saving a black boy." He stopped and wiped the wetness from his lips with the back of his hand. "Actually, at one point this was about a kid in Oklahoma stuck in a well. What's your point, Frankie?"

"His point's nothing," said the shaggy blonde at Pops' table. "He wants to try to impress us. No one buys it, so he changes the subject. That's his point as far as I can tell."

"I want to impress you?" I asked the kid. "Ask Molly Donaldson, if I wanted to impress you I'd buy you a drink and fall asleep next to you. Anyway, your precious kid's still in his well, you can go on sobbing over him. Meanwhile, the only man among us who's done a damn thing worth talking about is offering you a life lesson, and you're smacking my hand away."

"A life lesson," Pops said. "I got to get a lesson in life from a never married three-hundred-pounder with a half exploded liver." He turned to face Jesse. "Son, you're young enough to still make a bad decision and have it matter. I'll buy you a drink if you promise to me and everyone here that you don't trust this man's lies. Just please, restore my faith in America's young."

Jesse downed the last of his drink, and stood up. "You're forgetting," he said, "Frankie's my boss. If I don't offend him and get fired, then I can afford to buy a lot more drinks than one." He nodded to me, and signaled to the door. "Anyway, we got to get back to the cleaner's. Your brother told me to check here first, and if we're much later he's going to know we've been drinking."

"You've been drinking, boy," I said. "Not me. I've been patiently illustrating my superiority to the rabble here, each of which owes God at least one black child." I gave a half bow to the crowd in front of the T.V. "But, fellows, I'll leave you secure in the knowledge that you've done less with your life than the man you look upon as the town drunk."

The shaggy blonde stood up and pointed to the door. "You, out," he said. "Just go, man."

I put my hands up, shrugged, and followed Jesse out the door. The sun shone bright, dead in our eyes, and we both stopped for a second to get our bearings and readjust to the heat. The smoke from the house fire had thinned and mostly disappeared, but I could still smell where it used to be.

Jesse slipped another cigarette into his mouth, and grinned at me. I knew it was coming. Go ahead, kid, I thought. Break my heart. Ask me if I'm telling the truth.

But he just fiddled around in his pocket, and brought up a lighter. "That kid in Oklahoma," he said. "You know they're going to save him. They wouldn't have made it a national story if they weren't sure they could bring him up alive."

"Frankie," I heard someone call from behind me. Alex Hobbs stood with his hands on his knees, panting from running out of the bar. "Was that true what you said in there?" he said. "Pops said he'd buy me two drinks if I got you to admit you're lying."

I looked at Jesse, and gave a big sigh. Some people, I thought. You can tell them the story of your life, and all they care about is whether or not they believe you. "If you think I was lying about the black boy, then why'd you trust me to tell the truth now?"

Alex looked around, confused. "Pops said he'd buy me two drinks if I got you to admit you're lying."

"Fine," I said. "I made it all up. Be sure to get something expensive."

Alex rubbed his forehead. "So you was lying?"

"It's possible" I said. "And it's possible that the truth isn't worth one drink, let alone two."

Alex let a quick childlike smile flash through his sunken, hang-dog face, and ran back in the bar to collect his reward.

Jesse nodded to me, and started walking down the road, back to the cleaner's and I followed, having to almost run to keep up with his long legged stride. "You know," I said. "There was a fire on this mountain just this afternoon."

"I know," Jesse said. "I heard the sirens when I was coming to get you. I'd guess no one was hurt."

"No one?" I said. "How long have you been gone? The Fire Department can't get a cat out of a tree without killing it. You expect them to put out a house fire without anyone getting hurt?"

"Maybe," he said. He took a long drag of his cigarette, and blew the smoke up above his head. "But the only reason I can pry my eyes open each morning is that I only believe whatever I want to believe."

"How long have you been doing that?"

"About a year," he said. "It's not easy, but I'm starting to get the hang of it. Sometimes I forget, but not as much recently."

"I tried something like that," I said. "Got me sent to rehab a few times, but whatever keeps you going's all right, I suppose." I turned back to the bar to see if I could field any more questions, but the door stayed closed.

Steve Finbow

Mrs. Nakamoto Takes a Vacation

She fixes herself a bowl of miso soup, steamed rice, and pickled plums, and takes them on a tray into the living room to eat while watching the weather report on television. The day is going to be warm – a thin layer of cloud burning off by midday. Mrs. Nakamoto nods, finishes the last drops of her soup, fills a bottle with water, and leaves the house. The journey to the station takes fifteen minutes and she walks in her usual manner – small steps, head slightly bowed, turning her neck left and right and dipping her forehead as a greeting to people she knows, people she sees most mornings. The people do the same. Nothing is said, just the incline of the head and the muffled grunt of acknowledgement. But she doesn't recognize anyone this morning. Where is the man with the excitable dogs? Where are the schoolchildren eating persimmons? Where is the old man with the red umbrella?

..

The previous night, while alone in bed, sleepy but determined to stay awake until midnight, Mrs. Nakamoto decided to take a holiday. Noboru, her husband, had sworn he would never again go on holiday. He travelled the country yet refused to take Mrs. Nakamoto with him. She longed for the days of her childhood. Each year, until she was fifteen years old, her grandparents took her to Shikotsuko, a volcanic lake in Hokkaido. In the third year of their marriage, Mrs. Nakamoto had accompanied her husband on a business trip to Hawaii. Noboru spent his days at conferences and in meetings, his nights getting drunk in hotel bars. Mrs. Nakamoto sunned herself on the beach and shopped for souvenirs. The nights she spent eating alone in their hotel room waiting for Noboru to stumble into bed. It was to be their only vacation together.

She liked being alone. She didn't miss Noboru's stiff smile. She certainly didn't miss the smell of tobacco from his foreign cigarettes. He went away on business at least once a month, travelling as far as Kagoshima in the south and Abashiri in the north. For 20 years, Mrs. Nakamoto had listened to Noboru's travel stories, his heroism as a sales representative, his expertise at closing a deal. But during those 20 years, Mrs. Nakamoto was never quite sure what it was her husband sold. Their married life began in a cramped two-room apartment on the second floor of her father's house in Chiba City. Steadily, over the twenty years of their increasingly diffident marriage, they had inched into Tokyo, living in various apartments in Katsushika, Shibuya, a heavenly two-year stay in Noboru's uncle's house in Aoyama, only to be flung out by the centrifugal force of the city to the quiet towns of Saitama Prefecture – Kumagaya,

which she adored and, finally, Waco, which she toler-
ated.

A week ago, Mrs. Nakamoto went with her good friend
Hitomi Matsuda to the Tokyo Disney Resort. They
watched people on rides. They visited the Mystic
Rhythms show and spent the time giggling behind their
hands and whispering to each other. Later that evening
in an izakaya in Ginza over beer and yakitori, Mrs. Matsuda, slightly drunk, admitted to Mrs. Nakamoto that
her husband beat her. He would come home from
work, eat his food in silence, read the newspaper's
sports section and, after neatly folding it, would nod his
head. Mrs. Matsuda would strip naked, bend over a
chair and Mr. Matsuda, taking a three-foot bamboo
cane from the kitchen cupboard, would issue a dozen
lashes to Mrs. Matsuda's buttocks. Holding her glass of
beer in both hands, Mrs. Matsuda looked down. Mr.
Matsuda was a colleague of Noboru's. Looking up, she
smiled and in a voice Mrs. Nakamoto could barely hear
Mrs. Matsuda said that she was embarrassed to admit it
but, yes, she quite enjoyed it. Mrs. Matsuda winked and
then smiled for so long Mrs. Nakamoto thought her
friend had had a seizure. Mrs. Nakamoto said nothing.
At around 9pm, Mrs. Nakamoto and Mrs. Matsuda said
their goodbyes. On the way home, Mrs. Nakamoto
thought about Mrs. Matsuda's confession. What was
she supposed to think? She didn't know. But she was
sure of one thing – not once in the last ten years had
she smiled the way Mrs. Matsuda smiled that evening.

Keeping an eye out for cyclists on her way to the station, Mrs. Nakamoto enters a Lawson's. She's not sure
why these places are so bright. Men browse through

teen magazines. Workers examine sandwiches and instant noodles. Sales assistants, dressed in their blue and white candy-stripe uniforms, begrudgingly polite, wait to serve. Mrs. Nakamoto stares at the soft-drink selection not sure what it was she came in for. Then, high on the mountain, on the topmost branch of a tree, she sees a blue and green bird. It is singing. She strains to listen. The bird seems reticent, as if testing its newfound power. Mrs. Nakamoto is sure she knows the tune, recognizes the melody, the bird's voice is zithery, tuba-like, saxophonean, and Mrs. Nakamoto starts to hum along. It is *Moon River*. She closes her eyes, but the bird stops and she looks at it. The pied bird, now red and yellow, winks at her. I'm going your way, says the bird. Mrs. Nakamoto holds her hand to her mouth. Am I in your way? The shop assistant asks. Are you OK? Mrs. Nakamoto blinks. Mrs. Nakamoto nods. Mrs. Nakamoto picks up a chocolate bar and takes it to the checkout. After paying, she looks back at the refrigerator holding the cans of sugary drinks and wonders if the light reflecting on and in them caused her to see the bird, hear its song. Maybe it was the liqueurs. Maybe it was the whisky. Maybe she stayed up too late watching television. She nods to no one in particular and continues her walk to the station.

Noboru made love to her regularly and roughly. The house clocks set their time by Noboru's acts of passion. Gentleness was not his forte. Nor foreplay. Nor undressing, for that matter. It was as if the ghost of lust haunted him. It had him do its bidding but at a place separate from the bedroom; like watching oneself in a mirror trying to thread a needle. On the last Friday of every month, if he wasn't traveling, he would leave a note for her describing what she was to wear that evening when he arrived home. Promptly at 9:55pm, she would slip into leopard-print panties, black lace teddy, or his favourite, a pink, fur-trimmed, see-thru negligee Noboru had brought home with him after a trip to Osaka. She would slide beneath the covers and wait for the jingly ingress of Noboru's front-door keys. She sometimes heard him stumbling drunken from a cab, the soft thunk of the automatic doors, his faltering footsteps. These sounds were Mrs. Nakamoto's foreplay. Mrs. Nakamoto would slip her index finger into her vagina and make sure she was moist. As Noboru entered the bedroom, illuminated only by the small cat-shaped bedside lamp, Mrs. Nakamoto would nod. Noboru would pull back the duvet cover, unzip, and motion for her to get on her knees. She had long given up attempts to kiss him. His whisky, beer, and seafood breath would reach her, dampen her lips and, as Noboru entered her, she would close her mouth. Pretend. She would feel the negligee's cheap material tickle her lower back, feel his prickly pubic hair, his quaggy thrusts, and two minutes later it would be over and Noboru would close the bedroom door and within minutes be snoring on the living-room sofa, a can of Sapporo Draft in his left hand. Mrs. Nakamoto would touch herself again, turn on her side and, before sleep, before she turned out the light, she would draw an imaginary heart with an arrow through it on the darkening space before her. In that heart, she would etch her initials and those of the one she loved.

On reaching the station, Mrs. Nakamoto looks at the clock. Then she looks at her watch. And again looks at the clock. One hour early. But how is that possible?

Woken by the alarm, she took off her eye-mask, turned on the bedside lamp – the cat's eyes burned red, – raised herself on one elbow, sipped from a glass of water, sat up, and located her house slippers. She showered, washed and dried her hair, dressed in a dark blue suit, white blouse, a single string of pearls, and fixed her hair in a chignon, securing it with two black and red lacquered hair grips. She warmed her soup, finished her breakfast and left the house. This all took 45 minutes. Always. So, why did she have an extra hour? Maybe she set the alarm earlier. She was slightly woozy from the chocolate, whisky, and the perfumed warmth of her bed. But she distinctly remembered pulling out the alarm button. Maybe she had nudged the minute hand. She looks at the station clock.

If Tokyo's subway system is Orochi, the many-headed dragon, then the Yamanote line is the Ouroboros, consuming itself in its inner-city loop. To Mrs. Nakamoto, they are 'the serpent' and 'the worm'. Her usual journey to work is to take the Tobu-Toju line from Wako-shi station to Ikebukuro station, then travel on 'the worm' four stops to Shinjuku station. She is early. She decides to take the soto-mawari worm clockwise to Yoyogi Park, drink a coffee and eat a pastry in a small café, before walking the short distance to the Times Square building complex and the Takashimaya store where she works in the shoe department.

She goes over it again in her head. Why is she early? Noboru bought her a large box of liqueur chocolates and Mrs. Nakamoto spent the evening in bed propped up by two pink pillows, watching television, steadily devouring the sweets, her face covered in a mineral mud facemask. On the side table was a glass of Noboru's 10-year-old single malt whisky. An ice cube bobbed like a milky eye in the oily brass of the liquid. She flicked through the television channels and settled on a variety show. The gaudy set, the loud costumes of the performers, their striped socks, plaid skirts, and camouflage trousers, their dyed spiky hair, their garish make up, screamed out at her. She reached for the remote to turn down the volume, then smiled gently – her facemask cost ¥10,000 even with her store discount and she didn't want to crack it. She replaced the remote on the bed, stroking it gently as if it were an old and trusted lapdog.

Noboru Nakamoto, a thin, pinched man, had only danced once in his life – at a family party when he was 17. The DJ played *Rock Around the Clock*. A drunken evening here, a forbidden cigarette there, and, sometimes, when Mrs. Nakamoto was out with Mrs. Matsuda, Noboru would rent an adult video, pour himself a glass of whisky, crack open some dried squid, and watch the movie, returning it to the store before Mrs. N came home. Apart from his job, these were Noboru's only pleasures. And the last Friday of every month – of course. He would wake exhausted, a post-coital can of Hokkaido's finest in his hand, sneak a look into Mrs. N's bedroom – he snored, they slept apart – and nod to himself as she slept. He would tiptoe into the room and turn off the small cat-shaped lamp, which left a strange heart-shaped glow reflected in the bedroom window.

2:15am and all is quiet in the Nakamoto residence. Outside, cats hunting rodents and birds, cats scavenging from blue plastic bags, cats fucking in the yellow-white light of streetlamps. Cats traveling secret routes, defying gravity, sleek and battle-hardened. Inside, in the small hours, Mrs. Nakamoto sleeps and as she sleeps, the cats watch the rodents and the crows watch the cats.

The Tobu-Toju line takes Mrs. Nakamoto to Ikebukuro station. The train arrives and Mrs. Nakamoto gets on. It isn't busy and she finds a seat next to a man who is all elbows and knees and in a deep sleep. She places her hands on her thighs, squeezes in her shoulders, and makes sure her feet are together. Sitting to her left, a schoolgirl reads a magazine full of pop stars and actors. Mrs. Nakamoto can hear through the girl's headphones the crackle of instruments, the scratchy peel of voices. Stale air fills the carriage. Mrs. Nakamoto holds a hand to her mouth. Other passengers seem unaware of the smell. Mrs. Nakamoto loves the smell of crushed strawberries. She often carries fruit. In summer, bees court her, as do the wasps and dragonflies that hunt them.

The smell seems to be coming from the smoking cedar tree by the train's central doors. Flames lick up the branches. There are soft explosions of birds. Fire settles around the tree's crown. Mrs. Nakamoto looks at an advertisement for green tea. A mouth opens on a leaf and words come out quick and chaotic like shooed chickens. Mrs. Nakamoto cannot understand the leaf, the mouth, the words. The tree gives a loud 'shush', rustles its blackened leaves. On one of the lower branches, a charcoaled stump cracks open and from it, shaking its wings, steps the singing bird. It opens its beak, and above the roar of the train's wheels, the whoosh of the tunnels, above the schoolgirl's tinny music and the man's sleepy whistles, she hears *Moon River*. The bird thrusts its head forward and says, oh, dream-maker, you heartbreaker, says the schoolgirl and kisses a picture of a longhaired young man. Holding the strap above Mrs. Nakamoto's head, another schoolgirl, skirt riding high on her baby-fat thighs, looks away.

Approaching Otsuka station, the girl next to Mrs. Nakamoto rises from her seat. She and her friend cross to the doors. The girls are in their mid-teens. Their hair bleached a foxy red, their faces burnt orange and thick with make-up. As the doors open, both girls turn to look at Mrs. Nakamoto. Pointing at her with their long painted fingernails, they break into an impromptu kara-oke – two drifters off to see the world – putting their hands to their mouths, the girls giggle and stand knock-kneed on the platform. As the train pulls away toward Sugamo, they look at Mrs. Nakamoto, their faces tanned and their eyes dead.

She doesn't have to work. Noboru has asked her on many occasions to give up the job. She has argued that it gets her out of the house, it is only part time – three days a week – and that she has friends there. Mrs. Matsuda told her about the job. Mrs. Matsuda works in the toy department. Before working at Takashimaya, Mrs. Nakamoto spent the mornings cleaning and shopping, and the afternoons watching television or reading a book – thrillers usually. Bored by this, Mrs. Nakamoto smiled when Mrs. M told her about the part-time position. It meant commuting but she thought she would enjoy that. She didn't go into the city often and she could read during her journey. It had been years since she had had an interview but she wasn't nervous. She had some retail experience having worked in a book-store when at university, she also had a large collection of shoes, and a good knowledge of the different design-ers, makes, and prices. She thought she may be slightly too old for the position but the managers who inter-viewed her were impressed by her experience, her appearance, and her willingness. They asked if she could start the following week, and work Wednesdays, Thursdays and Fridays, and she said she could and she did. She didn't tell Noboru until he came home from a trip to Fukuoka the Friday after her first week at the store. He mumbled. He grumbled. She brought him a beer and a newspaper. He seemed placated and, al-though he mentioned it from time to time and urged her to give it up, he didn't push, and he didn't moan. She enjoyed her work. She liked shoes.

Mrs. Nakamoto looks up. What has she been doing? The train is approaching Ueno station. She cannot re-member it stopping at any of the stations, nor can she remember passengers getting off and on. Maybe she worked a little too hard this week. She covered for Mrs. M in the toy department on Tuesday – Mrs. M was vis-iting her daughter in Kyoto – and volunteered to work long hours on Wednesday and Thursday to help with the stocktaking. Noboru was away most of the week, returning yesterday in a foul mood, dumping his brief-case and drinking the best part of a bottle of sake. She stayed up late most nights watching television. That is it. She is tired. That's why she is early, why she can't concentrate, why she keeps thinking of that forest, that… Mrs. Nakamoto's hand moves to cover her mouth as she thinks of the word…bloody bird. Too much sugar in those chocolates – that's what caused her to wake early.

The train empties and fills. Salarymen nap on their way to the office. Tourists stare at the subway maps, unsure of their direction, popeyed and gaping from the push and shove of Tokyo mornings. The man sitting next to her lurches to his right and bumps against Mrs. Nakamoto's shoulder. The man on her left thrusts his arms out in order to read his newspaper. Mrs. Nakamoto pushes her spine into the chair to get a little more space. The man on her right snores and Mrs. Nakamoto smells his soupy breath, beer-tinged, with an undertone of tobacco. The man on her left works his elbow, digging it in to her ribs. He stares ahead oblivious to her discomfort. His breathing is rapid, almost panting. Mrs. Nakamoto looks down at her knees. Under the pale sheen of her tights, like two fog-shrouded suns, she sees two red circles. Sitting opposite her, a young girl, dressed incongruously in a pink negligee fringed with white nylon fur, sings to herself, We're after the same rainbow's end, waitin' 'round the bend, my huckleberry friend, Moon River, and me, and as she sings she smiles, her tongue plays over her white teeth. The girl closes her eyes and tears appear and her mouth opens again, the tongue bloody and swollen wiggles in her now toothless mouth.

Tokyo Station. The lake, fringed by boulders, caresses her skin in its strangely warm waters. She sees the swan-shaped boats bobbing at the shore. The peaks of the volcanoes silhouetted against the night. She is naked. The water holds her steady. Her head and shoulders glisten above the surface. She feels the depths beneath her, almost solid. Feels the valleys and mounds, the weed fields, the fish. The man to her left folds his newspaper, places it under his arm and stands to get off at Shinabashi.

Mrs. Nakamoto looks at her watch. The station's platforms blur by. She wants to be at a table in a small café near Yoyogi Park sipping at a latte, picking at the buttery flakes of a croissant. What is happening to her? She looks between the two women sitting opposite her. In her reflection, as smeared and greasy as the window, she can make out her pearls and, when she smiles, her teeth, her red lips. Above her head, a plume of steam drifting off from the mountainside. The moon, palmed in the expert caress of the clouds then unpalmed, paints the tips of trees, boats, and waves.

Mrs. Nakamoto closes her eyes. She hears the soft thunk of cab doors and men's voices. Two sets of footsteps and drunken laughter. The bedroom door opens. Two men appear. Both in suits, both swaying in the doorway. The thinner of the two enters and gestures to her. She rises and kneels. The man unzips and pulls her pink panties aside. Enters her. She feels his thrusts. She closes her eyes. The man runs his index finger between her lips, brushes against her teeth, opens them with his thumb. Her mouth fills with flesh, she looks up at the man's protruding belly, his shirt undone to his navel, his tie stroking her forehead. She feels the man behind increase the rate and harshness of his thrusts. The man in front of her holds the back of her head, pulls her to him, and then away, matching the rhythm of the man behind. She feels his pubic hair tickling her chin and nostrils, and then her mouth fills with him. The man behind withdraws and a dribble of warm liquid runs down her left buttock. The bedroom door closes, the front door slams, the refrigerator door opens, and she hears the sharp crack and hiss of a beer can's pull-ring.

Mrs. Nakamoto opens her purse. She flips open her cell phone. 08:00. She tries to catch a glimpse of the other passengers' watches, but bags, coats, or newspapers conceal them. As the train pulls into Shinbashi station, Mrs. Nakamoto looks at the platform clock. It reads, wherever you're going, I'm going your way – 08:00. A fish leaps out of the lake onto the bank, thrashing and gulping. A cat pads toward it. A crow planes down from a branch. The fish is still. The cat nods to the crow. The crow nods back. The cat extends its claws and hooks the fish's mouth. The crow does likewise with the fish's tail. Slowly, and silently, the two ease the fish back into the lake. Once there, it shakes itself, pushes its head out of the water, winks and flashes down into the deep.

Gotanda, Meguro, Ebisu stations flash by. She wipes herself with tissues she keeps in a box on the bedside table. She places her hands over her eyes and sobs. Her negligee, ripped and stained, lies on the floor beside her feet. She dresses in a toweling robe. She opens the bedroom door. To her right, she can hear laughter coming from the television in the living room. She stops by the kitchen door, thirsty but not wanting to make a noise, she places her mouth under the tap and turns it slowly. The water is cold.

Yoyogi Station. Mrs. Nakamoto remains seated. Probably best to go straight to work, she thinks. Have a coffee in the staff cafeteria. Be near people. Maybe Mrs. M will be there. Maybe she should call her from the station. Ask her what she thinks is wrong. Passengers begin to stir as the train approaches Shinjuku, gathering bags, buttoning coats, folding newspapers, all accompanied by coughs, splutters, and sneezes.

She stands behind the noren at the entrance to the living room. A man's hand trails beside the arm of a leather sofa. She can hear gentle snoring. With her right index finger she separates the curtains. The man's thin face, drawn and grey, sweats and twitches. The top button of his trousers and his flies remain open, as does a packet of dried squid on the table in front of him.

The lights of Shinjuku station fill the windows and Mrs. Nakamoto sees the commuters three-deep on the platform waiting to board the train, each face a blur, and then clear, and then whipped away from her. She hears the announcer and the ping-pong of the doors. She sees the haphazard ranks of the trees, of vines, and bushes. Hears the bird's song. She feels the tickle of tatami under her feet, the polished knob of a drawer. Hears her breath, calm and easy. She sees the station slow into sharpness. She hears the doors' electric whoosh and the dry whoomp of geese wings. She hears the whistle of metal and leather through air. She sees the train slowly empty and a woman step onto a faraway shore.

James Lawless

Jolt

Standing in a soft cotton towel, the night air caressing him like a heating fan, he looks out the open shutters of the veranda. He hears the waves breaking on the shore to the haunting chant of the muezzin echoing over the minarets and onion domes of the mosques. To the west a huge globe of sun is setting. He looks back at his wife sleeping, her head partly covered by the sheet, a sleeve of her white nightdress sticking out, revealing an arm as if dismembered. He listens for her breathing, not loud as it sometimes is, but gentle now, in harmony with the waves.

Is it sixteen or seventeen years now since they first met at the Galway literary festival? His love of books, her love of singing pubs and *craic*. She liked to give the impression she was a bit of a bohemian with her loose sweaters and jeans, or 'off-duty' denim skirt to replace her starchy nurse's uniform. Bought him the *Faber Book of Irish Verse,* which he read to her, said he read beautifully, finding Yeats a turn-on, he captured the emotion, the pathos of the poems in what she called his 'mellow Dublin voice'. She was passionate, demonstrative in her lovemaking. 'Oh a nurse, is she now?' Flaherty in the bank had said, 'they can make you come in thirty seconds flat. A slight puffiness around her knuckles now – she uses soap to remove her rings before going to bed.

They had no honeymoon. After the wedding it was back to Dublin. She nursed in the Maternity hospital in the Coombe; he worked in a Phibsboro bank. All their savings and energy were being put into the building of the new bungalow on the half acre of ground that Michael had perspicaciously bought some years previously in Meath.

Two years after they married they had a baby girl, Niamh, the darling of their lives. She grew tall (Michael's long legs) with dark pigtails (her mother's hair). During the Easter break of her first year in secondary school, Niamh went on a school trip to Belfast. A bomb exploded in a pub as the tour bus drove up the Grosvenor Road. The bus, its windscreen shattered, careened out of control knocking down a schoolboy before coming to a halt on the pavement. Niamh and two other girls, who were sitting on the pub side of the bus, and the boy who was knocked down, were pronounced dead on their admission to the Royal Victoria hospital.

Kathleen never went back to work after losing Niamh. 'Could *you* face it?' she said accusingly to him. He wanted her to try and go back after months of moping, sitting in her dressing gown at the kitchen table into the late afternoons, smoking cigarettes. It was depressing to commute through the heavy traffic every evening and arrive home to see her still sitting there listlessly in the same position. He avoided kissing her. 'What did you do all day? 'I painted my arse red and went mad,' she said, 'what do you think I did?' 'It would get you out of yourself,' he said, 'if you went back.' 'What? Go back to all those other babies?' she said, scratching furiously at the flaky skin on her left arm. 'No way.'

She drew deeply on her cigarette, soggy between her lips. 'Before Niamh I mean I could look at those other babies, at their weak chests, their umbilical hernias, their defects, but they were perfect for someone. That's what a baby is, isn't it, Michael, a little thing with a defect to be nurtured whole.' She sighed, lifted a strand of tobacco off her tongue. 'There we were on the conveyor belt handing the striplings over with their half closed eyes in their little shawls and Moses' baskets to their doting parents. "A perfect little darling," I'd say and all the time knowing they were not.' She was sobbing. 'Niamh had a hernia, remember? Do you remember?'

Things started to slide, like the cooking, the piling up of unwashed plates; the same happened with her appearance, she didn't care; her breath smelled; her dandruff returned. 'Too much heating,' he said, 'you always have the central heating on; it dries up your skin. She feigned a shiver. 'Does it occur to you that I might be cold?' 'You shouldn't stay indoors so much,' he said. 'You should circulate the blood.' 'You want me to go out, is that it?' she said irately. 'I'll go out.' She started going to a pub where they sang nationalist ballads, and a bodhrán player thumped out her sorrow.

Michael felt the strain. Damn it, he wasn't just a reinforcer of another, he thought one evening as he sat waiting for his TV dinner to heat in the microwave.

What did she expect of him? Every day coming home tired from work trying to find new ways of consoling her. It was exhausting. There were limits to what a partner could do, could keep doing. 'You have to put things behind you,' he said. 'Things! How can you call Niamh a thing?' 'I'm not calling Niamh a thing. Disasters,' he said, 'whatever, you have to put them behind you.' 'Did you not see the body, the lacerations...? Have you forgotten already?' 'Of course I haven't forgotten, but it's three years now, Kathleen.'

Three years became four and five, and there was no sign of any more children forthcoming. If only they could have another child to prevent the ghost of Niamh from creeping back, from dominating the forefront of her mind, night and day. Were they destined to wallow in a lifetime of sorrow? It wasn't fair. She was using him merely as a weeping sponge, an emotional turn-screw. Every time the news came on the TV with mention of the North, she broke down. She had a box of man-size Kleenex on the coffee table beside her couch, and she would grab a fistful of these tissues whenever the need arose to quell the flow of her tears and muffle the sound of her wailing. He told her to go and see someone, but she took umbrage. 'Is that what you want?' she said. 'You want me to go and see a shrink, to be a laughing stock.'

He didn't pay much heed to the singing pubs that she dragged him to in the beginning of their relationship. What were a few rebel songs? He actually enjoyed tagging along, enjoyed a drink. The songs were harmless anachronisms. Sex was the thing. She'd get high on the vodka and the music. She'd slobber over him. He didn't mind when it led to something more. What guy wouldn't? She sneaked him into her room in the nurses' home, and got naked with the sheets pulled back and the light from the moon through the window painting her thighs silver. 'Come to me now.' An order. And when he came she would say, 'Good boy,' as if he were a child who had done something wonderful.

It was fine, a novelty to have a woman so...so uninhibited until in time, not long into their marriage, he began to grow a little tired of some of those initiatives, like the way she'd always throw herself at him, tearing the clothes off his back the minute they'd get home after work. 'Oh, the traffic,' he'd say, just wanting to sink into an armchair and unknot all those snarling juggernauts and complicated accounts from his brain. There was no time (or inclination) for arousal, no time to unwind, no time for anything gradual. That was Kathleen. She cooked fast, would 'throw' something on the pan; made love fast, her thick hair wet with sweat, tossed back like a mane, and she in the throes – 'There now, good boy.' To her, sex was like eating a bread roll or chewing gum, just a habit, nothing much to be made of it, but part and parcel nevertheless of what in some unwritten code she was expected to do. A female must service her male, it's a primeval thing, an irrefutable behavioural pattern of animal attraction.

She sang loudly; the national anthem she stood to attention for, at the end of each ballad session '...and Ireland long a province, be a nation once again.' There was a lack of finesse in her, that's what it was, he concluded cruelly, what distinguishes the human from the primate.

But all those qualms were quashed, knocked on the head, when Niamh was born, and eleven years went by of near normality. They now had an outer object of affection, a repository of unconditional love as they were fused together for one purpose. They decorated and painted their bungalow, took a real interest in their half acre garden. It was formerly just a sweeping lawn, not without its share of thistles and dandelions which Michael felt duty-bound to mow whenever its length dictated. But now all of that was to change. Kathleen planted spring bulbs to bloom in time for the baby's birth. Michael took some time off work – free days that were long overdue – and built a chain swing and a little sand playground far back from the road. So...so safe. He closed his eyes, damming the incipient flow of a sly tear.

Kathleen in the hospital paralleled the lives of all the babies with that of Niamh. She would look at tiny prehensile fingers and pudgy noses in a new light; tickle under chins to elicit the big chuckle, to get babies to show off their dimples (like Niamh's) and she'd go singing, 'Where can the baby's dimple be?' She studied every nuance of their child's development. Sometimes she used the possessive *my* even in front of Michael, forgetting to say *our* child, but he didn't mind; he understood; she was just getting a bit carried away like all new mothers do. She kept records – the first golden lock of hair, every cough, the type – in Niamh's pink baby book. 'Who can tell, but in some future time she may need to know if she had the whooping cough or measles.'

The waves of the Aegean crash on the rocks, indifferent to time, keeping their own time, thinks Michael, as early light streams through a glaucous sky. Someone in a distant room starts up an electric drill. She stirs, turns towards him, yawns.

They were different: rural west, urban east but open, open he liked to feel. No baggage, that's what he said, and she thought he meant for travel purposes because that was their last topic of conversation before deciding something was needed. 'A jolt is what we need,' he said, meaning to her of course. A new environment, a sea change, a holiday, a belated honeymoon, call it what you will, there was a need for such a thing. 'To save a marriage,' he said in a final exasperated tone. It was a Sunday afternoon in early spring when he said that, five years after the death of Niamh. Kathleen was still in bed flicking through a glossy magazine. He knew he'd struck home because normally she'd continue flicking irritatingly while he'd be talking to her, his words just flying over her, but this time the flicking stopped. She scratched her head, the snow of her dandruff littering the page. 'As extreme as that?' she said.

They chose Turkey, or rather Kathleen chose it from a coloured brochure she picked up in a travel agents in Liffey Street, and Michael agreed. It had an exotic ring: Islam, belly dancers, camels, the desert, Istanbul. The veil over the eastern world. Before they went to book the holiday, they had heard of isolated incidents of rebellion. It was on the news: the Kurds looking for independence. It brought it all back to Kathleen about the North. 'Maybe we should go somewhere else, Michael.' Michael sighed. 'We need to go somewhere far if it's to do the trick. It's no good just going to some Costa Blankout to meet your neighbours from down the road in their timeshare apartments.' And the travel agent assured them, one hundred and one percent safe; those isolated incidents were far away from where they were going.

The flight, a long four hours, was tiring but not enough to assuage their night ardour in a rattly hotel shower. 'It's come back,' he said. It was the travelling, being forced to look out for each other in their high adventure. 'Did you write the arrival address on the suitcase sticker?' 'Have you the passports?' A new alertness, a practical caring, distance forcing them out of a former despondency to be mutually dependent. It was something basic, primeval, yes, thought Michael, that is the word – and he savoured it on his tongue like a sweet or a good malt whiskey – in a land they knew nothing of: different language, religion, climate. 'Oh Michael,' she said, as jets of steaming water cascaded down her breasts. 'This is what we needed, isn't it, ISN'T IT?'

They sit in the breakfast room under huge chandeliers glittering in the early sunlight which is streaming through the high windows. Could they fall? wonders Kathleen looking up at the shimmering crystal. 'They're so heavy looking, Michael, what would happen if they fell?' 'They won't fall,' says Michael. Those fears, he thinks, she never had those fears. Phobias.

They meet Hazel and Aubrey, a couple from the North of Ireland who, to Kathleen's annoyance, plonk down at the same table in front of them. 'We're next door to you,' chirps Hazel and she commences to sing 'Neigh...bours,' imitating the TV soap. Michael laughs but his laugh quickly changes to a muffled grimace at Kathleen's under-table kick. Hazel is pleasantly plump, making her look older than she probably is with a sort of maternal grace. Aubrey's muscled biceps peep through his short-sleeved shirt. He is touching on the low in stature with mousy, thinning hair. Hazel is the talker, takes an immediate shine to Michael, and Michael, perhaps flattered, warms to her *joie de vivre*. He likes the way she doesn't take offence when a waiter enquires if his 'mother' is requiring anything.

'Mother,' she exclaims good-humouredly and then with a wink she says, 'We heard you two in the shower.'

'How could it happen?' says Kathleen after the couple have left for the beach. 'Our luck. You'd think it was on purpose. Let's get out of here, Michael.' 'We can't do that,' he says, his shin still smarting from her kick. 'Let's change hotels at least.' 'Every place is booked. It's high season you know.' 'Did you try?' She's shaking him, making his muesli regurgitate in his stomach. 'You're just saying that.' 'Look, Kathleen,' he says firmly, removing her hands from his shoulders, the same hands that held him in such a different manner only several hours earlier. He looks directly into her distraught eyes. It's a time to be firm. They had made a decision. He feels he's playing the psychiatrist, the person she should have gone to see in the first place. Repressed memory, all that sort of stuff; some people carry it with them all the way from early childhood, some thing buried deep, crippling the person, and all for the want of a little aeration. Mulrooney, his anal-retentive boss is a bit like that, come to think of it; never said anything that was his own. What a psychiatrist could do with him. 'How is the trouble and strife?' he'd say which was a handy way of not remembering a wife's name. Oh for some spark, some fire to drive out fire, he thought. 'Look, Kathleen,' he hears himself saying, his voice sharp like a psychiatrist's fingerclick breaking a trance, '*they* may be exactly what you need.'

'You do this to me, take advantage of me,' she is saying as they walk along the plush-carpeted corridor to their room, indifferent to a couple of fair-haired Swedes who smilingly stand aside to let them pass. 'How am I taking advantage of you? You tell me,' he says. 'You are,' she says, starting to whimper, 'taking advantage of our being far away from home.'

He knows from past experience the futility of continuing to argue with her when she is like that, totally illogical, he thinks. It would be like rolling out a string with bigger and more entangled knots. He hears her gargling in the bathroom, using the beaker, giving her mouth a thorough rinse. Is it coming back, the thoroughness, the former perfectionist in her? She was never really bohemian except perhaps in the sex. She was someone who couldn't let go of things. Niamh, the perfect child, moulded into her likeness and then... violently rent, hard to accept, he accepted that.

It was an *umbilical* hernia, he remembered, Niamh suffered from.

He hears her snapping her toothbrush into its plastic holder. 'Those people,' he says through the chink in the door, 'you can't blame them.'

They are climbing a hill, a goat's path. It's early afternoon, the sun vertical in the sky. She is wearing her blue denim shorts. He looks at her as she climbs ahead of him, her milk-white legs never looked quite so pale back home. Three or four goats appear and start following them. They frighten him as they get closer with their horns, bells tinkling. She laughs at him. He's embarrassed. Kathleen knows goats. They had them on the farm in Galway.

She sheds her shyness in the open countryside. She wants to make love *al fresco*. There is no one about except for the goats. She breathes in deeply the fragrance of the pines. Lying down on the scorched earth, she loosens her blouse, drawing him into her. 'Is it possible,

Michael? Say it's possible.' She stares up at the sky. Blue for a boy.

During the evening meal, however, Kathleen, recidivistically continues her sullen appraisal of Hazel as she banters with the waiter. 'It's a communal table, we've no choice in the matter,' is Michael's whispered response to her complaint about having to sit beside the Northern couple again. 'Look around you. Can you see any other table vacant. Well, can you? You can't just get up and walk away.' 'Why not?' 'You can't do that sort of thing, Kathleen, and remember what I said to you about them earlier. So just relax, will you.'

Aubrey says nothing. He's not a speaker, she concludes. He smiles in a slightly bored way. World-weary. He orders more wine before the others have finished theirs.

Hazel puts down her fork, the last morsel of sherry trifle impaled on a tine. 'I enjoyed that,' she says, dabbing her lips with her linen napkin. 'It's not the same,' says Kathleen argumentatively 'as the ones back home. The sherry tastes off.' There is a moment of awkward silence making the background sounds of other people's voices and cutlery and plates come to the fore. Michael pushes his bowl of unfinished dessert towards Kathleen incriminatingly. Hazel says, 'I wasn't always so....' The three wait for the sentence to complete itself... 'so round.' 'She wasn't and all,' says Aubrey who is scraping his bowl apparently indifferent to culinary nuances. So she *was* offended by that waiter's remark after all, thinks Michael, or was it the silence just now that had made her uncomfortable, forcing her to think of something fast to say, even if confessional? 'Do you ever...?' says Hazel. 'What?' says Michael. 'Oh no,' she says, 'you wouldn't. Men don't. Maybe...' She transfers her gaze towards Kathleen who is in the process of trying to squeeze her napkin back into its silver ring. Michael wishes she would desist. It's a nervous action. Why can't she leave it for the waiter to do? 'Do you ever binge eat, Kathleen?' says Hazel. 'No,' says Kathleen. 'Well I do.' 'She does and all,' says Aubrey.

Kathleen is about to ask her why she'd do such a thing, but that is exactly what she wants her to do, she concludes, looking for attention. Isn't that essentially what binge eating is all about? So, she won't bother. Why should she give her any satisfaction?

Hazel, 'the unflappable', thinks Kathleen, is talking about a boat trip she saw advertised on the notice board in the vestibule of the hotel. 'It's to an island on a lake. Would you be interested?' Michael, withstanding Kathleen's withering dart, says, 'Sounds like fun.'

Michael wonders about Kathleen; when will she bring it up about Northern Ireland? It's only a matter of time before she ignites the fuse, but maybe he's wrong, maybe she will give these people a chance eventually if he perseveres. He was always on about that, taking people as you find them, although it was hard at times with some of the bank crowd; but when you'd meet people casually, it cost nothing to be friendly. And these Northerners, you can't tar them all with the same brush, and Kathleen knows that. Tarred and feathered, maybe not the right words. Inflammatory. But at home Kathleen talks vehemently about the North. She always did, even before Niamh, but now she has become pathological. She is an expert on timing devices. She can tell from what range and what angle a bomb is lethal or not.

..

The trip across the placid water – glistening azure – takes less than an hour. They pay the ventricose boat-man who takes visible pleasure in helping the ladies disembark, brushing his hand rather obviously against Kathleen's denimed buttock.

'Let's get a shot first,' says Hazel excitedly, 'over by the bougainvillea,' and Kathleen finds herself sand-wiched between Aubrey and Michael, being forced to smile into Hazel's camera lens. It could be a bomb, the click. She is going mad.

They sit by the lake near a ruined masjid. Hazel opens a wicker picnic basket (the hotel arranged it). Aubrey uncorks the wine. Linen napkins. Tuna salad, oysters on ice. 'What did *we* bring?' whispers Kathleen into Michael's ear. 'Relax, we're guests. Next time, okay?' Next time? Hazel makes sucking noises with her fingers in her mouth which Michael finds sensuous. A tactile person, he thinks not unlike what first attracted him to Kathleen. 'What's the book, Michael?' enquires Hazel. A slightly worn paperback was jutting out from his small haversack. *'An Answer to the Enemies of Islam.'* 'Where did you get such a thing?' 'At the bazaar in the town.' 'And what does it say?' asks Hazel. Michael flicks through the pages. 'It's not a laugh a minute.' 'Tell us,' says Hazel coquettishly. 'Well, it says stuff like each century will be worse than the one before until Doomsday.' 'Oh no,' says Kathleen, 'that's all we need to hear.' 'Good holiday reading,' quips Aubrey. 'The writer seems to think,' continues Michael, 'that spies are everywhere undermining Moslem belief; but there are some nice poetic bits about the stars leading you to fe-licity.' 'Ooh Felicity,' pipes Hazel mockingly, 'who is she? Let me see.' She moves closer to Michael. 'For God's sake,' says Kathleen, and she looks to Aubrey who, to her dismay, is smiling on.

There's a festival. Lots of fireworks lighting up the night sky. Lots of boom (Kathleen thinking it is the Kurds) frightening the street camels laden with their pots and pans and carpets, and all sorts of market paraphernalia becoming undone, holding up the hooting traffic. 'Watch out for pickpockets,' warns Aubrey as they find themselves being pressed by the throng. Kathleen breathing hard, panicking slightly, as her autonomy gives way. Hazel's reassuring voice. Laughter. 'You okay, guys? Isn't this something?'

They are led by a Turk, bearded, turbaned, through a maze of side streets to be shown carpets. 'Exquisite designs, all done by hand. Wait till you see.' 'Once it's not his harem,' says Hazel laughing. They go behind veils into a dark grotto surrounded by silks and coloured cloths of different texture and carpets of course, hundreds of them all rolled up. 'Which is the magic one?' enquires Hazel saucily, 'Ali Baba's?' The Turk laughs. 'Please sit.' They look for chairs. There are none. An old woman crouched in a corner smiles toothlessly at them. They sit on the ground, balancing awkwardly as they try to bend their legs into themselves in the Turkish fashion. They are served tea in tiny glasses. 'Irish?' says the Turk. 'Yes,' says Kathleen. '*Póg....mo...thóin,*' he says proudly and raises his glass.

They return to the hotel on a crowded dolmus. 'What did the phrase mean that he used to toast us?' asks Hazel. 'Kiss my arse,' says Kathleen venomously, delighting in the opportunity to dramatically direct the translated words at Hazel. 'Some Irish tourists pulling his leg,' explains Michael. The Irish women scream as the bus lists to one side when the driver takes a sharp bend at speed. The drop is sheer, straight down to the sea. The native passengers look on in silent resignation, their torsos and heads rocking in sync with the movements of the bus. 'If we survive this,' shrieks Kathleen, 'we'll survive anything.' But Hazel is not smiling this time. She is out of her seat balancing herself precariously on the floor of the bus and loudly berating the smiling, uncomprehending driver on his recklessness. 'Don't you realise...' she shouts, 'I say don't you realise people could get killed.'

There is the sound of a distant explosion as they unstick themselves from the bus. Kathleen, startled, snuggles into Michael, her beach dress riding up her thigh from the sweaty seat. 'The end of the fireworks,' says Hazel (her composure restored). 'Are you sure?' says Kathleen. They link arms, the four of them, at Hazel's prompting, as they mount the steps to the hotel. The strap of Kathleen's bag, with her piece of bought carpet sticking out, keeps slipping from her shoulder, affording her the excuse to break the chain.

They take a trip to Ephesus – a long journey on a coach provided with a knowledgeable Turkish courier with impeccable English. The best preserved city of the Roman eras. Better than Rome. The great city, the famous library, the tunnels up to the brothels, the cobbled streets still intact, the commerce, the shops. Michael tries to imagine the hawkers of the ancient world, the traffic, centurions and slaves and of course Saint Paul. 'The Virgin,' the courier says, 'retired to a place near here.' 'They don't believe in her,' Kathleen murmurs, referring to Aubrey and Hazel. '*They* don't either,' Michael retorts curtly, 'they're Moslem re-member, but they still relate the story.'

Someone asks the courier about the explosions and the Kurds. He lowers his voice even though he is still speaking into the microphone. 'Yes, there were explosions. Those people...' he hesitates... 'they are being denied their ethnic rights. Hunger strike.' Kathleen nudges Michael. 'Ask them what they know about Bobby Sands.'

Her mood swings like a pendulum. No, she cannot deny that they appear nice people, but everybody is nice on a holiday. It is fine, everything is fine when the subject is roses. There is a jollity, a universal merry-making *de rigueur*. But the dark side keeps returning to her, the cold side as it does now forcing its way through like a cloud, a blemish in the searing sun and heat of a Turkish summer. Forcing its way through the pale blue sky, the colour of the Virgin's cloak.

Water spills from her plastic bottle, which she had left down on a pillar of the great Alexander's library, the water frizzing into nothingness in a matter of seconds. 'Fry an egg on the stones. An Ulster fry,' quips Hazel. 'She means an Irish fry,' whispers Kathleen into Michael's ear. 'I bet she says Londonderry too instead of Derry.' The heat rises as if it has muscle punching them in the face. An elderly man in the group faints. People are burning up. They are applying and re-applying high factor sun creams to pink flesh. How did people work in such a climate? It is unrelenting. No shelter. Ephesus ruins. How did such a city throb with life?

They are put up in a hotel in Pamukkale in the interior of the county – the trip too long to return the same night. The mountains look snow-covered but it's the lime, and the pools' hot springs which sprout up all over the place have medicinal qualities. Old people with folds in their skin are gently swimming.

The four of them swim or rather float, for the water is so full of salt and lime and minerals it is impossible to sink. It is a solemn place where, according to the courier, people concentrate on healing their bodies' ills. 'Just the body?' says Kathleen. 'What?' says Michael, but talk is drowned out by Hazel's squeal as she splashes in the water. She is wearing a dress swimsuit with navy polka dots, and a little frilled canopy covering her wide haunches.

They make love with the shutters open to the light of the full moon. He laughs as she says she was at sixes and sevens in that foursome.

'That makes seventeen,' he says.

'Stop making fun of me, Michael.'

'What about the goats?'

'They're Unionist.'

'The goats?'

'Michael.'

'They're okay,' he says.

'How can you say that? They torment Catholics.'

'How do you know what they do?'

'Their names.'

'How can you make such insinuations?' he says angrily. 'Ask them. Have it out with them if you must.'

'Mind,' shouts Hazel, pulling Michael back onto the kerb as they make their way down to the beach the following morning. The dolmus whizzes by. 'They don't even slow down.' She looks deadly serious. 'Fucking buses,' she exclaims, the sudden profanity jolting Michael.

The beach – a small rectangle of dark sand – is as

crowded as the streets. Kathleen rummages in her car-
rier bag for her sun cream, and her hand brushes
against the little leather purse – more like a case for ro-
sary beads it is so small – a birthday present from
Niamh. She always carries it with her even though she
uses a bigger wallet to hold her passport and traveller
cheques. The little pouch for Mammy, bought with her
own pocket money. Her last year...how did Michael put
it? 'before she was shuffled off this mortal coil.' Eleven
years. She was boasting she was now a teenager in Irish,
aon bhlian déag: déagóir. Strange, the Gaelic precocity over
the English. In some things. Niamh was a good Irish
debater. She won the best speaker for 'Peace is coming
through', about the North of Ireland. She practised her
speech on her mother. She talked about the dove, vul-
nerable like white paper on an ocean wave, and she
would look up from her notes from time to time, as she
had been instructed, seeking eye contact with the audience. Pick someone to focus on, and she picked out her
mother sitting proudly in the front row. And Kathleen
took the photograph which she is looking at now – always kept in the little purse – of her daughter standing
as team captain in her wine uniform with the silver cup
in her hands (a silver chalice, she thinks religiously for a
moment). The North of Ireland. The irony of it. She
was so sweet-tongued, her Irish words were like honey
on her lips. Kathleen felt so close to her, closer perhaps
than she was even to Michael. Was she fooling herself
in that regard? Would it have been different when she
became seventeen or eighteen? But Kathleen liked to
think that she would have been able to take all of that
on board, whatever changes were to be. She would have
been vigilant. She would have anticipated like Michael
does or tries to do on most things. We *were* so close, she

ponders, tears welling. She steals another look at the photograph (Michael is busy reading). The pigtails tied with white ribbon and the dazzling blue eyes. *Her* eyes almost, although hers were more grey, but certainly not Michael's. The smiling face; the long summer-tanned legs with the white ankle socks under the school skirt, growing too short already. The local boys beginning to give her the eye. Oh, she noticed. The beret slightly too small for her womanly brow. All beginnings. A little shudder.

Hazel and Aubrey are disrobed and in the water splashing about noisily like children. Kathleen, wakened from her reverie by Hazel's high-pitched scream, says, 'You'd think they'd act their age.'

Michael frowns but says nothing. He has put his book down and is happily looking out at the swimmers, sharing in their jollity. He does not want another argument, especially not in public. He looks around the beach. Homer, Heraclitus, the courier spoke about them, said they lived around the area. Imagine them as your next-door neighbours. Life, a permanent flux. Couldn't be more true. Knew what he was talking about, that guy, Heraclitus, with all the babel of noise and multi-ethnic toes and naked breasts practically touching strangers on a beach. And in the middle of it all two dark skinned guys throwing a frisbee.

Kathleen, wriggling the sand under her towel, hands her Nivea 15 to Michael to do her back. 'Do it evenly,' she says.

She settles belly-down with her magazine, occasionally adjusting her white cotton sun hat which appears too small for her head. The frisbee strikes her arm. An apology in a strange language. 'No damage,' says Michael. The guys – in their twenties perhaps – smile and resume their play. She looks at him. 'What do you mean, *No damage*?' she exclaims, rubbing her arm. The coolness between them is still there from the night before. 'Well?' 'Well what?' 'Why don't you say something to them?' 'It was an accident.'

That night she does not make love to him; she is tired; her arm is hurting. She is still peeved. The tap on the arm leads to a diatribe against Turkish men. The way they treat their women, their harems, disgusting the way the women have to go around all covered up in this great heat. Those grids on their faces like the man in the iron mask.

'Burkas,' he says.

'What?'

'That's what they call them.'

'Cruelty is the proper name.'

He glares at her. 'You're so negative. Why did you choose Turkey if you feel like that? It was *your* choice, remember?'

'Oh Michael,' she says softening, 'what are we doing, tearing at one another like this?'

'You're doing all the tearing.'

'Stop it, will you?' She is shaking his shoulders. 'Can't you see it's those two who are doing this to us?'

Mid-morning finds Hazel and Aubrey sitting at a table by the bamboo-canopied pool bar. They are drinking from tall slender glasses, domed with red cocktail stick umbrellas. Hazel's arms have a smooth even tan, her sallow complexion adapting comfortably to the sun. They wave as Kathleen and Michael appear. 'Do we have to go over to them?' It would be rude not to.'

'We were down in Galway,' Hazel is saying. 'We

had come down a few days early to do a little sight-seeing before our flight out from Dublin. We like Galway, don't we Aubrey?' 'Aye, we do,' says Aubrey. 'We stayed in a wee hotel in Ayre Square,' says Hazel. 'You know Ayre Square?' 'No, we don't,' snaps Kathleen.

'Condescending that's what they are,' she says later. '*We love Galway.*' 'She didn't say that. She said they *like* Galway.' 'And coming down to Dublin to save on their sterling. They'll be taking over the country next, those Northerners. Just look at RTE.'

Their lovemaking is suffering. Excuses for avoidance are more common now. Is it possible after such a short time? Maybe if they took a break from Hazel and Aubrey for a while. Maybe if she confronted them, as Michael suggested, spoke directly to them about her feelings, about Niamh. Would they listen?

They go out for a candlelit dinner, just the two of them. An expensive restaurant near the harbour. Lights from the yachts illuminate the inky surface of the ocean. A figure-hugging black dress subdues her sunburn, and her shampooed hair, shining auburn in the candlelight, smells so clean. She smiles lovingly at him. It's as if she has been hoovered out, he thinks. Her mind cleared of all the petty thorns that pricked it in the past. She holds his hand, plays with his fingers, his wedding ring, rotating the gold. The perfectibility of the world veiled by candlelight. And he thinks of the women veiled. And wonders is this the only way the world can work, soft focus reality. They talk gently, the wine bubbling inside them. Purring sweet sounds into each other's ears. They play footsie, her espadrilles thrown off, her toes caressing inside the leg of his chinos. Her hand goes under, fingers dancing along his thigh. It had all been a misunderstanding, the whole thing. The polite cough of the waiter. 'Will there be anything more, sir?'

That's when Hazel and Aubrey arrive, just at that moment when the waiter makes his enquiry. 'Great minds,' Hazel says, hugging each of them in turn (Kathleen remaining rigid), and then, as if remembering herself, adds, 'You don't mind?' They pull up chairs without waiting for a reply. 'What have you ordered?' They order the same grilled sole. 'And the wine?' She lifts the bottle to read the label. 'We'll have that too.' 'Jesus Christ,' Kathleen whispers audibly.

'What a day,' Hazel says, laughing into the candle-light, 'and here we are now finding you.' As if it's a reward, thinks Kathleen who is becoming increasingly irritated by Hazel's constant billing and cooing with her husband. And touching – too often has she touched that arm of his. That's a wife's domain, her domain. Is that how these Protestant hussies carry on? Have they no respect for the sacrament of marriage, or for themselves? They could be swingers, wifeswappers, the way she made that lewd reference to the shower. She looks at her husband. Oh Michael, you're a lamb for the slaughter. Her Michael, hanging on that tease's every word. What is she talking about? Some inanity, some triviality. Binge eating! She would stop at nothing to get her way. There she goes flashing her false eyelashes at him. She has to admit Michael is handsome, but she never told him of course. It's not a thing to do. You don't tell a grown man a thing like that. Might lose the run of himself. Handsome in an ascetic sort of way; the chocolate brown eyes, the high cheek bones, and svelte figure; never had a weight problem, Michael, the same waist measurement every year when she buys him the new slacks for his birthday. Maybe she could have varied the present an odd year, come to think of it now, but Michael never complained. The way that hussy is looking at him, she could swear she's giving him the come hither. It's blatant. She looks across at Aubrey, at his bloodshot sclera. He is helping himself to another glass of wine without, she might add, offering to pour for anyone else. What does he make of it, all this canoodling? He has to notice. Is he a man at all? Hazel is squeezing Michael's arm, pretending to make a point. Kathleen tries to console herself with the hotel waiter's words that she looks like his mother. Old, old, ha, she smiles. But she's taking a better tan than her. Damn her. In the candlelight she looks...she looks almost attractive.

'Oh, the things that happened to us today,' Hazel is saying, her fat jowls moving. Could it be goitre? Kathleen wonders hopefully, all that flesh underneath her chin? 'We were having such fun. We got a taxi. A safer driver than last time, wasn't he, Aubrey?' 'I'll say,' says Aubrey. 'We got out at a quiet beach. I mean let's face it, the beach we were at the last day was...a bit crowded.' 'A bit!' says Kathleen, unable to restrain herself, 'it was like a sardine tin.' 'Oh, and the statue; remember the statue, Aubrey,' says Hazel. 'Aye,' says Aubrey, 'Ottoturk astride his horse.'

'I never saw the sea so blue,' says Hazel, 'turquoise.'

'It *was* turquoise,' says Aubrey.

'And the beach, loads of room,' says Hazel looking towards Kathleen, 'beautiful silvery sand, and guess what?' she says with a twinkle.

'What?' says Michael.

'No, guess. We went up the beach. Guess what we stumbled upon?'

'A tortoise,' says Kathleen.

Hazel bursts out laughing. 'A tortoise.' She pulls at Michael's sleeve. 'Your wife, Michael, she's ... a hoot.'

Kathleen glares. How dare she...how dare she refer to her as *Michael's wife*, as if she...were not even present.

'A nudist colony,' says Aubrey, putting an end to the charade.

Hazel clasps her hands. 'Could you believe it? I mean could you believe it?'

'You joined in, I take it?' says Kathleen sarcastically.

Hazel stares at Kathleen. A puzzled look. Michael feels uneasy, wants to say something.

'We started to swim across a little channel,' says Hazel resuming. 'The current was strong, but the Swedish couple helped us. They waded in, didn't they Aubrey?'

'Aye,' says Aubrey.

'They're beautiful. The Swedes.' She smacks her lips.

Night evokes more sexual ardour from Kathleen, as if her passion is restored, or maybe she was turned on by the story of the nudist colony, or maybe she just feels the need to make it up to him. She had been a bitch. Her own words. 'It was nice of you,' she says, stroking his hair. 'What?' 'To pay the bill.' 'We owed them.' There was no need, she agreed, to take her dislike of the couple out on him. Michael is right, we carry baggage in all our dealings with people. There's no such thing as a clean slate, so we have to work on these things. 'Michael.' She opens his trouser belt, feeling a suffusion of love towards him. She straddles him on the wicker chair in the veranda. Michael wonders will the chair support the weight of both of them. He feels uncomfortable; he feels it could collapse at any moment. Something is catching at his left buttock – the silver belt buckle – but he can do nothing about it. Grin and bare it, as they say. She groans under the black starless sky to the hum of cicadas and the spray of the watering hoses. Just the little wall light to see by. 'Where has the moon gone? Tell me the poem, Michael. Recite it to me about the moon,' she says rocking him, her exposed breasts bouncing. He supports her by the hips, balancing her. 'Tell it to me, Michael.' 'Pluck,' says Michael, 'till time and times are done...' 'Don't stop. Don't stop.' '...The silver apples of the moon, the golden apples of the sun.'

But in the morning Hazel and Aubrey are like intestinal worms eating into her. 'I blame you,' she says, 'we were doing fine on our own until they came along. We were having a private dinner. Why didn't you tell them to go away?'

'Because I didn't want to, okay? You don't *talk* to them. You just sit there and find fault.'

'Find fault?'

'Yes.'

'You're asking me to talk to them? They're godless. You saw the way...'

'How do you know what they are?'

She looks at him, tears in her eyes, pleading with him for understanding.

'I'm sorry,' she says. She reaches out to him, touches his hand.

'Look...' he says, but adds nothing.

In the evening they walk down the darkening streets, she linking him, hugging in close to him. They stop to throw coins in a little begging girl's bowl.

'See her fingers,' she says, 'Michael, they're in a cast.'

She stoops down to the girl to examine her fingers. 'What happened to you, *girseach?*' The girl grins, her teeth radiant through the dark skin.

'She's probably a Kurdish child, Michael,' she says as he draws her away. 'Her parents could be dead.'

'They break the fingers by stomping on the hands. I read that.'

'Oh Michael.' She nestles into him clearly troubled by the young girl's plight. 'These are the things, Michael. These are the things.'

She rushes back to the girl and places paper money neatly folded into her bowl.

Kathleen holds tightly onto Michael as they make their way through the crowds, the sound of the hooting cars and buses only now becoming audible, only now entering her consciousness. She shivers despite the great heat. That little girl would only have been Niamh's age.

A crescent moon is shining through the open shutters as she slips from under the bed sheet. The crescent moon, she remembers Michael saying, the cross of the Moslem. She looks over the veranda, the moonlight striking silver on her nightdress. She glances back into the room. He is sleeping. He turns slightly, perhaps sensing her absence – a vacancy in his dream.

She will talk to Hazel, have it out, is that what Michael said? She will tell her about Niamh, make her know, make both of them know that Northerners' troubles can spill over other people's lives.

She walks along the corridor, or rather glides ghost-like, soundless, barefoot on the plush carpet. There is singing – the last hoarse notes of the night – rising from the bar below. What time is it? She has no idea. Is it too late to call on them? Maybe she should go back, talk to them in the morning, but she feels a compulsion in herself now, that she knows she may not feel tomorrow. The door of their room is ajar. Had they forgotten to close it? Were they too drunk? Most likely. A shaft of golden light shines out through the crevice of the door. A sound of sobbing. She thinks of knocking. Instead she pushes the door gently forward. Aubrey, with his bare back to her, is sitting on a sofa, cradling Hazel in his arms.

'I'm sorry,' says Kathleen. They look around. 'I couldn't sleep. I...'

'It's all right, come in, come in,' says Hazel, sniffling. The rims of her eyes are red. A side of her hair is matted, and a beard of cream rests on her chin. 'The door...' says Kathleen. 'We left it open because of the heat,' says Aubrey, who is dressed only in his wine-coloured pyjama bottoms. Hazel taps the sofa seat on her free side. 'Sit here beside us.'

She sits down nervously, conscious of Hazel's sweatmarked nightdress fallen now from her shoulder, exposing an ample breast. In front of them is a low table covered with cakes and sweets and sweet wrappers and – the subject of their gaze – a framed photograph of a young boy, perhaps eleven or twelve with dark brown eyes in a blue school uniform.

'Your son?' says Kathleen. She's about to say, what a fine looking boy when Hazel starts to sob again.

'A holiday is no good,' sniffles Hazel. 'We try. How we try. You have seen us trying, haven't you, Kathleen?'

'Yes,' says Kathleen, not quite clear what she is affirming but anxious nonetheless to empathise with another's sorrow.

Hazel dabs a tear with a large tissue. Aubrey looks at her solicitously, and pulls another tissue from a box and wipes the cream from her chin. He kisses her on the forehead. She reaches for an éclair and swallows it whole.

Kathleen sits with them, staring at the photograph in wordless vigil and, to the sound of the waves crashing on the shore, she touches Hazel's chocolate-stained hand.

Lee Joans

Vaselino

Miles and Elfie hadn't even seen the corpse, though they'd waited in line twelve hours. And now Elfie was bleeding from the left wrist, her body limp in raw silk, in Miles's arms. The sure force of his thumb, the slowness of his pace in the windless heat meant, by the time they'd arrived back at his lodgings, Elfie had clotted. Paused at the entrance their combined shadow formed a strange figure, humped-backed, long fingered. It fissured through the asphalt for a second, only.

Next day on the railroad platform, waving Elfie off back to Elkhart, Miles would recall that crowd outside the Frank E. Nesbitt funeral home: fifty thousand people in lowered-hat repose. Then without warning a rumbling underfoot like a great anger boring up through the earth. Silence into sound. A riot. Briefly, the memory roused him from his depression. He watched as the Lake Shore train carriages pulled away. Elfie's face was a stoic palsy. Staring past him, as though hexed, she did not wave. Soon, her features shrank to a dot. Miles exited Grand Central searching his palms, palms pricked with sweat; he hadn't known a summer hot as this one since '23 and he'd never know another.

In the lobby Elfie's blouse hung open, ripped. At her décolletage the skin was lacy with the dried blood of several cuts. Miles averted his eyes, forming a human crutch to take most of her weight so that her feet danced the stairs en pointe. His palm cupped thigh: there was no other way to lift her. Her silk dress was barely a barrier, he thought, between them...loose around her like a skin shedding. And damp, dark, sweat-puckered blots all over.

As they reached the landing, Mrs Tuttle and her little dog appeared blocking their way. Both she and the pug had in common a set of features that seemed to congregate near the chin.

'Just what in hell's name is going on?'

At the sound of the landlady's voice, Elfie's eyelids fluttered to reveal only their whites. Momentarily, Miles felt like a puppeteer as he propped Elfie's jelly spine upright, and, supporting her one-handed, turned up her cloche hat revealing to Mrs Tuttle her satiny forehead. As he did so Elfie's astonishing violet eyes flashed open, then shut tight. In that second Miles noted an unspoken exchange between the two women, which seemed to bridge the fifty years between them. He had, though, become tired of noting life's subtleties like a secret hoarder.

Despite having established the girl was not in danger, Mrs Tuttle tongue-lashed Miles anyway: 'I had warned you, Mr Staksis, about joining those schmucks. Peeping Toms! Who'd wait in line to see a corpse that wasn't their own blood family?'

The corpse, Rudolph Valentino's corpse, was two days' dead of a perforated appendix. The minute she'd heard, Elfie had cycled to the platform at Elkhart, her trunk secured with twine across the bike's front basket. Today had been their last opportunity to view the body, pay respects. Street fighting, an overturned Ford Sedan and jealous, mostly male, snickering about the Great Lover's miniature manhood – in the file-past – had put an end to public viewings. In September Valentino would make his final train journey, not to Italy, never again to Italy, but to a Hollywood mausoleum. Innate in Miles, impossible to voice, was the certainty he was different to the other thousands waiting, that he, too, would be significant. Their line had advanced so slowly. And despite many anxious searches while Elfie talked in his ear, he had not picked out of the crowd another man like him. A Vaselino.

Vaselino was his umpteenth christening since he'd come to Manhattan. After Milos Staksis came Miles Monroe. Staksis would close doors for him. So Miles Monroe was the autograph he'd practised daily, until lately. So, in acting class, after *cake-eater* and *flour lover*, after *pink powder puff* – *Dago futz* he thought he'd heard, too, one time – after all the names that slayed him, came Vaselino. Progress. Acceptance. Somehow he'd conjured Valentino in their heads and as nicknames went Vaselino was perfect, the eel's hips – as Elfie used to put it. Elfie had confirmed that million dollar something in him, years before. 'The wind blows through you different, Milos.' – she'd said that, before he'd moved out to this city. Had leaving killed it off?

Regarding the question of Valentino's corpse, Miles made to answer Mrs Tuttle. She quashed his voice to a whisper. 'Mr Staksis…' Her vein-knotted hand took hold of his chin, 'You'll find your clown face is melt-ing…I ask what is this world coming to when our young men are afraid a' showing their real faces…'

Miles transferred Elfie to lean against his left thigh while he fumbled for his room key. He nodded once to Mrs Tuttle; aflame with a shyness, which, once it took hold, had the potency of horror. His insides had gone kapoosh at her mention of his real name, and in antici-pation of the sight of the panda eyes – the black kohl slid into white greasepaint – that might greet him in the mirror.

Mrs Tuttle hadn't spoken much in the past five years – though she always appeared on Elfie's visits. Mostly, all Miles heard was her bolting and unbolting the locks up and down her room door. Occasionally, he'd see her carrying out scraped plates from meals consumed privately. From snatched glances of her cherry chaise longue, her single porthole window, her feathered full-length dresses and the smoke of her El Rey del Mundo cigars lingering in the hall – not to men-tion the absence of a Mr Tuttle – Miles had pieced together her private world, her mode of being.

And Mrs Tuttle was sure about Miles. Regularly in-tercepting his mail, she hand-delivered it, re-sealed, to his room. *Mr Milos Staksis* his mother's perfect script read. Mrs Tuttle read that Mother respected his need for a stage name – Miles Monroe – but he would always be her Milos. Had Mrs Tuttle not removed, in a rare flash of guilt, the most recent letter from the steaming pot, she might have been chastened to learn of Miles's aunt Gladys's winter months spent in Los Angeles State Institutions.

Since June, when aunt Gladys had given birth to a daughter, Miles's mother, Mrs Doreen Monroe-Staksis allocated half of every letter to the pros and cons of uprooting West. *I fear for little Norma Jeane's best interests,* Doreen wrote. Miles, who had a recent fear of small babies, could summon only bland advice in his short reply; the coded subtext of which screamed for her help.

Mrs Tuttle's breath was on Miles' collar. She loaned her broad shelf of a shoulder to assist him in putting Elfie to bed. At the weight of patchwork thrown about her, Elfie lashed out. In an eye's blink, Mrs Tuttle had exchanged it for the thinnest gauze invented. Meanwhile Miles tugged up the sash and ushered in air with his palms for the sake of looking practical. There was no air. He couldn't wait much longer to check his appearance in the mirror.

For the benefit of his landlady, while they both stood watching Elfie breathe, Miles began explaining how she had sustained her cuts. A crowd-surge. The storming of a plate glass window that shattered over folks' heads. Panic. An old lady stamped on, shoes minus feet, a child… He stopped, aware of his voice rising, his accent slipping, colloquial with fear and unselfconscious excitement.

Mrs Tuttle cut him down. 'Put a hundred men in any kind of heat and you'll get bloodshed and hysteria. Now help me set your lady friend straight. She's coming to life.'

Miles dragged Elfie up the bed onto Mrs Tuttle's soft crucifix of pillows. The manoeuvre called for intimacy. Contact with Elfie's cold wet armpits shot currents through his forearms. Mrs Tuttle stood poised to help but soon stepped aside redundant, a little speechless at his strength. His action was a moral blend of duty and brute force: these days Elfie was close to six feet – near as tall as he was. More and more on her bi-annual visits she seemed all limbs; all breasts. But her legs had lost their tree climbing muscle of old, Miles thought.

The only other time Miles Monroe had lifted a woman had been during rehearsals. A corny, only mod-erately censored, adaptation of Sister Carrie – so his wallet clipping from Amateur Theatre Review had it – for which Miles had understudied for the part of the young salesman, Charles Drouet. Naturally he'd tried out for the Hurstwood part – it still gnawed at him, too. At least with Hurstwood he felt, he could have brought a little magic to the role.

Hurstwood, who dies alone in a down-at-heel New York lodging.

Halting one of the Charles Drouet scenes Mr Polorow rubbed his cheek and said: 'Son I dunno where you're from but we gotta knock it outta ya. Fluidity is the key. No leading lady's gonna wanna end up bruised. Let's go. Try again.' Second take, Miles lifted Carol Ann to grudging applause from the class. But back at Mrs Tuttle's that evening Mr Polorow's advice confused his head; it being in direct contradiction to his mother's written encouragements:

> You're a fingerprint Milos. You're Unique. Every human being on this earth is just a set of breaths between two dates. Remember to celebrate your life, son, and keep trying and don't let them tell you who to be. Meanwhile your checks are ever helpful regarding household expenses. Oh I called in by the butcher's shop Friday for the brisket, I told Elfie I'd pass on her best wishes.
> Yours,
> Mother.

··

In recent months, celebration had not been on his mind. Returning home to Elkhart, a failure, had consumed him. After endless mental travels in which he pictured himself arriving home, resuming his place in the familial ring around the radio, Sundays, with Mother, Alexa and Nik, he'd concluded it wouldn't do to get sentimental. Five years on, Alexa was a wild middle child who arrived home unsteady, evenings – sometimes, Mother noticed, with a bruised neck. And young Nik, Mother feared, was nowhere near as thoughtful-minded as when Milos had been present as mentor. They'd grown older. Light-heartedly, his mother wrote him that Alexa gave her devil looks. Signing off, she wondered if perhaps Christina was burdened with the same disease that was pestering the mind of her sister Gladys.

Now the earliest of his mother's letters was translucent from lonely fingering. It lay flattened inside an otherwise un-thumbed birthday gift of Dos Passos' *Manhattan Transfer* (A gift from Elfie. He'd glanced at the first page, too dazzled by its modernity – Modern, baffling, was exactly Elfie's taste, besides which the mere word *Manhattan* always struck a bell in her head and sent her hand to her purse). Plus Elfie would always arrive in Manhattan – though this time it had been too short notice – with one of his mother's plate peach pies. Every goodbye, it was a kick in his lungs to see the cleaned down, blue-rimmed china being wrapped in cloth and taken back. But he could not go home: the simple fact was his mother, his siblings, might starve without his Plaza bellhop checks.

The fact he'd never watched a sunset here in the city

cured his melancholy a little. Sunsets happened on the other side of the building. Here in Manhattan, there seemed to be a zillion horizons – for all he knew the sun slid down the grates. Back in Elkhart the sun sank in full view of townsfolk's windows, like a great fire taking hold of the field, the silhouette of Marvin the bull like the devil on all fours.

Elkhart again. Elkhart, always.

For reasons Miles could not fathom, memories of his childhood connection to the earth had been coming like bullets to his lungs since early June.

A Ladybird: a surprise tickle on his upturned wrist.

Long grasses pricking into his navel, his stirring belly.

Afternoons lying on his back, a portcullis of shadow across his newly shaved chest.

Exhaustion by proxy watching ants busy on a stone wall.

Pruning the hideous clematis coiled around his father's headstone.

The thin, high notes of a white-throated sparrow. The same, shot, bird, dead, in cloth.

That last summer at home and his fourth wasp sting. Cousin Elfie busy with tweezers. 'You're prone to stings, Milos…the wasps must really love you a lot.'

The earth seemed to be calling him. Yet he'd never been interested in the earth. Since the age of 16 life had been about rooms and mirrors. Cool shelter. An interior life.

Mrs Tuttle was out on the fire escape attaching nets to the line-and-pulley. Once hung, they obscured the view of scores of other back room windows. The bottom of one net billowed in through Miles' open sash where it lolled damp and listless.

Elfie was stirring.

Though she wouldn't remember details she had inhabited most of Miles' daydreams in the past few minutes and was now murmuring her way out of them, tussling with her sub-conscious. Her fingers gripped the straggly fox fur beside her and she snatched it to her chest like a comforter. Waking made her grumpy, period. She could feel her chest and wrist pitting. She hung on in dream, for Milos was the smiling figure on a wood jetty in a warm place she didn't recognise but occupied with certainty, like a womb.

In the corridor, Mrs Tuttle called for her dog, just outside the open door.

Awoken, Elfie tried to stare through the gap. She sniffed deep and grunted. All that waiting and they hadn't even seen the body! She'd traipse back to Elkhart without so much as an anecdote; she'd trod on the hem of history, was all. Though, she didn't mind too much: Valentino was only ever a convenient cover and, lately, she hadn't cared too much for his oeuvre anyhow. Same old, same old. Not that she'd wish death on anybody.

She shut her eyes. Because when she opened them properly this rare feeling of control would be gone and the weary business of sleeping arrangements and return train schedules would rear up.

In the family trunk (Elfie its sole user) she'd carted half a drugstore, sacrificing precious clothing space. Since spring the trunk, packed expertly, had nested under her bed ready for her Fall trip. Each night of the countdown to the train ride she'd check through her accumulated stash, powder stacked on top of glutinous scar cover, either side of tiny tins of mascara and rouge. She scoured the Ladies' Home Journal for anything new and sliced pig, weekends too, until she could afford to pay for it. Oh, she understood what Miles needed her for. But she hoped it might develop, refine itself, back into love, given time. Because Love had been there, that last summer. And she'd noticed improvements over the past six years, sure. Little signs. She didn't itemize them: she distilled the happy essence from each event and pressed on with her devotion. Very special moments, on the other hand, made their way into private verse and fiction – heavily disguised, of course. The last story she'd written, the last story she would ever write, entitled Dark Silence, took place in a cinema. In it, the head of Kent De Savery rested on that of Delphine Turner. The detail of Kent's heavy skull, his navy pomade leaving a greasy stain on Delphine's blouse was, at the last minute, included – omitted – then included again – for its daring realism.

She wouldn't be pushy with Miles – though pushy was very much part of her bearcat self. The one time she'd forced a kiss from him, though he'd responded well and right, the residue was something sad. She'd made it happen: in future she'd make sure things happened to her. Afterwards in the soda shop they pushed away the empty coffee cups of the ghost couple before them and sat in squirmy silence over two dishes of brittle meringue. Well, at least she hadn't gotten the icy mitt: he'd kissed back. And hard.

Right now, she felt sour and stricken with the thought that, by coming to Manhattan on the hoof, she'd forfeited her usual Fall trip. Might another trip be too much, too soon? Miles hadn't spoken of future plans for so long.

Rolling over, she sensed his face close to hers. For a second his fingers touched the fox. Elfie bared her teeth a little and inhaled through her mouth. She heard Miles back off, his shoes on the floor, then, distant.

One of her problems in Miles's presence was that her real self, her invulnerability, was difficult to jettison. Also, the lexicon of youth was a ball and chain; she would have liked to impress with passages of Tennyson but she always defaulted to jokes and curses. Now, despite the time being right to level with him she sat up and sang raucously – a few lines from Send me to the 'Lectric Chair, startling Miles who was busy at the mirror. He laughed.

To keep him on his toes she stopped fooling and spoke to the mirror, which contained his back. 'Made you up nice didn't I?' He returned to his reflection, switching his profile from side to side with pursed lips until she laughed. Eyes like Mesmer's she would recall, in her final hour on the train.

'You shoulda left the Cupid's bow on, Milos…Suited ya… or maybe this city's not ready for a man with red lips…Hell…I'm sore, Milos.' She joined him by the mirror's ellipse. 'Next time I fall under a heap of men on the sidewalk, you leave me there.' She punched his shoulder, absorbing, via her knuckle, his muscle, sinew, and somewhere under all that bulk, his bones.

Their spirited exchange turned to low chatter and faraway stares. As it grew dark they sat either side of a bowl of water and anointed each other's faces with cold cream and a shared, hot, muslin rag. While Miles dried his face Elfie glimpsed the base of his spine, honeyed against a white vest. Honey: he looked like honey – even though he despised honey and olive and buttermilk. Feared the terms. Oils and greases. Words not far enough removed from the taunts in school to be at all complimentary. On the audition circuit they equated him with villainous roles, with The Orient, with Arabia, places he couldn't even point out in an atlas. Elfie looked at him, preferring his skin without the greasepaint. Like beauty glimpsed through rayon, she thought.

Miles had negotiated the usual room across the landing, beyond the stairs. Elfie took Miles's bed, a few inches longer than her own back at Grandfather's, it fit her. In the morning, she'd take the earliest train to Elkhart. That night, for the last time in Manhattan, both she and Miles slept. In fact, of the three on their landing, only Mrs Tuttle lay awake and fretful. She'd forgotten to bring in the sheets from the fire escape. Now rain was braying on the roof.

Towards lunch the next day, Mrs Tuttle fitted her wig and went to the fire escape to gather the laundry. Ridden with black fly at their corners, rain sodden, the sheets would not do; she'd have to commence the hand wash all over again, have them out and dried and folded and cupboard-stored by dinner. The hem of the last sheet was trapped in the open window of her young Mr Staksis. Mrs Tuttle tugged it free, resisting the desire to inspect the room. She limped back to the exit door, thinking how much she'd miss the presence of Mr Staksis' gawky visitor who came on the train twice a year. There was something of her estranged daughter in the face of that kid. Often, she'd wished a more solid companion for the girl: none of the young actors they ever sent to her lodge house had amounted to anything. Saps, the lot of them. Vain. Like watching bluebottles, she thought. Hell bent on battering thick glass when there's a wide window waiting.

If Mrs Tuttle had maintained her usual habit and peeped inside as she retrieved her laundry she would have noticed, from the blessed comfort of fresh air, the splayed out body of Miles Baker, his throat blood soaking into the grain of the floorboards, swamping Elfie's dried red flakes from the day before. Instead Mrs Tuttle saw it two days later from her airless lodge house; a whining dog at her feet and a handkerchief pressed to her gasping face. By that time, the severed limbs of Elizabeth Elf had been removed from the railroad at a point between Grand Central and Elkhart, the tracks cleaned down in preparation for September 2nd 1926 when the Valentino funeral train commenced its four-day journey West.

The destination of the funeral train was Los Angeles where, in a suburban hacienda, many miles yet from Sunset Strip, Miles's aunt, Gladys Monroe Baker Mortensen, woke to yet another bad day. Examining that day's mail, she sifted the envelope with her sister's shaky script and placed it top of the pile. For later. Not now. There was a storm in her head today, no room to crowd words into it just yet. Time passed. Eventually, when she stood, her leg bashed the table and she pinched the skin of her temples while her pale blonde, three-month-old daughter bawled for attention. Gladys Baker held her own arms steady so they wouldn't shake. She moved to push her head inside the hood of the crib of Miles' baby cousin. She asked, evenly, 'Are you frightened, too, Norma Jeane?'

Seated at an early screening of the Jazz Singer, Mrs Tuttle remarked to her companion Iris Polorow that there would never again be a place in the world for Valentino and his silent ilk. During the newsreel they discussed the unfortunate Staksis boy. The anniversary was coming round already.

It was a gross journalistic inaccuracy in the Elkhart Bugle that Elfie's death was an accident. Tumbling from the viewing carriage, she'd changed her mind about suicide. Subsequently, her chance at posterity depended on the manuscript of short fiction she'd submitted to McClure's Magazine, being culled from the pile, making contact with the fingertips and sensibility of one Eliot Johnson.

At the breakfast table, that hot summer of 1926, Eliot Johnson tugged out his tie knot and succumbed to a fatal coronary event. Three years later, McClure's shut down. Back in Elkhart, Elfie's grandfather turned over the last issue in his hands before double-checking for her name.

Forty years later the feminist author Harper Snaider Lancer raked over Miles's life for her book on Marilyn Monroe. Twice through in the New York Public Library she watched a restored reel of his appearance in Mr Klein's Chorus Line. Miles appeared smiling, for two-minutes-thirty.

> *Feminine*, Lancer noted in her margin.
> *Considerable cinematic presence.*
> *Obvious resemblance to M – smile etc.*
> *One film and three plays.*
> *No known recording of Staksis's voice.*

Nicholas Hogg

Paradise

*M*ercy Lang *crawls on her hands and knees between the naked men and women. She apologises to the bodies for asking them to move, but twice a day she has to wash and scrub each and every wooden slat of the sauna. She wears pads like a skateboarder to protect her knees from the flagstone floor. Guests at the Black Forest Lodge, awkward with their nudity in the company of someone clothed, ask her if Kenya gets this hot. They know Mercy is from Kenya because it says so on her name badge. She smiles for tips when she answers and paints them a pretty picture of Africa, sunshine after rain, steam rising off a melting highway, banana leaves limp with humidity.*

But this is a memory. It is now 2012, seven years since she has been home to Mombasa, eight years since she has seen her children, and ten years since she buried her first husband in the hills of the Great Rift Valley.

Fancifully, she likes to compare this kind of sweat and heat to the exertion of giving birth in a hut of clay and straw, the jubilation of life, Kembe and Lana, the son and daughter she has not seen since the day she caught a plane to Germany and married a man she did not love.

***

My mother was not as beautiful as the other prostitutes, but she levelled a pool cue as though aiming the barrel of a gun. She was as patient and poised as an assassin, leaning across the bright green baize of the table and sighting her shots, snapping the air with a crack when she fired.

And some men in the Paradise liked this more than a young girl in short skirt or flimsy dress. Especially the white men sweating through their suits, the fat men with shiny baldheads, the scorched men with pink noses, all watching her play, as were my brother and I, as though she were the last woman on earth.

Mother would wait for Kembe to fall asleep then kiss him on the forehead. She would tell me to be a good girl and take care of my brother. Sometimes she promised to buy me a new dress in the morning before locking the door of the apartment and leaving her scent in the room like a guardian spirit. I would try to climb from the second floor window alone, without waking my baby brother, not wanting him to know certain things about his mother he could not yet understand.

But if you share a bed that dips and rolls two into a single dream, then an eyelid lifting becomes a quadruple action. And anyway, his cries would wake the whole neighbourhood whenever he woke up alone.

By stepping off the ledge and onto the wall that stopped the stray dogs peeing in our yard, we could balance our way to the bar without ever touching the ground. We stepped between the shards of glass cemented into the brickwork, across the shacks of corrugated tin and over the Mombasa bus depot roof before dropping down onto the columns of stacked barrels at the rear. Unless one of the staff popped out with a crate of empties, or we came across a couple banging against the rickety fence like cats in heat, we had made it to the Paradise without being spotted by a neighbour or rounded up by the police as street children.

We skipped across the barrel tops and scampered up and along the higher branches of a mango tree to where we could peek between the leaves into the bar. The sign said Paradise, but nothing I ever saw in that room made me think of this word.

You could tell if white men were there or not by the pitter-patter of chatter and laughter that fell from the open windows into the streets below. No white men, no noise. Nothing to see except mother lining up the pool balls and cracking them into the dark holes of the pockets.

When it was busy the men sat crowded at the bar waiting to be served. If not drinking ice-cold beer to stop from melting, they eyed up girls on the dance floor. The way the younger women draped their bodies over the men, plucking bills from their grip like petals from a flower, I realised what power I would grow into, what power my mother was growing out of.

But playing pool she was Queen of the bar. She strutted around the table, curling her long fingers around the cue, blowing chalk from the tip with pursed lips and waiting for one of the white men to take up the challenge.

Kembe cried if mother lost, but I knew better. I knew if she lost at the start of the evening she would win the last game. And the money. Sometimes the men were angry, throwing the lost bet on the table and calling her a "hustler." I explained to Kembe this was someone who pretended they were bad at a game so they could win later. My little brother thought this was stupid. "Why?" he whispered to me in the treetop. "She should just win and come home sooner."

If she did lose, which was rare, or if the white men guessed she was a hustler before the bets were placed, she would go back to the bar and sit on one of the high stools. When she did this Kembe would start crying and I would have to muffle his sniffles and wipe his face with the hem of my dress. He knew then that she would not be home until morning.

First she would cross her legs, letting her skirt ride up over knees, showing the shining thighs she had rubbed with coconut oil before leaving the apartment. I used to watch her get ready in the cracked mirror, transforming from our mother to a stranger, another woman painted onto her lips, drawn around her eyes and massaged into her skin.

Then she would smoke, not because she liked to, as she never did at home, but so she could ask a white man for a light. The other women, mostly younger, slimmer, with extensions in their hair and shiny dresses that shimmered under the lights, smiled and giggled when the men lit their cigarettes. Mother bent to the flame with a look on her face as though she could reach into the soul of a man and pull it from his body.

And the men that wanted their life in her hands bought her drinks and gave her cigarettes. She did not paw them like the other girls. She did not laugh at their bad jokes. She whispered in their ears, ever so lightly brushed her body against their big stomachs, trailing her breasts along their arms and shoulders. When they reached for her, she looked away, across the bar, as though she had forgotten about their very presence. To reduce a man to nothing but the woman he wanted was talent the younger girls did not yet have.

The men she played pool against laughed and smirked when she first handed them a cue. But this was good. The bigger the smile, the bigger the bet placed. And lost. They broke and split the pack, flexed their muscles, knowing nothing of how to make the white ball spin, dance and shepherd colours into the pockets. My mother was too cunning to show them how great a player she really was, in the first game anyway. When she did loose off a spectacular shot, the bullet white picking off a stray, or maybe just a precision pot in slow motion, the men quickly realised defeat, counting out their money before the black dropped into the clunking machinery of the table and sealed the end of the game.

We wanted to clap out loud when our mother won, but if she saw us dangled in the treetop watching her work we would not be able to sit down for a week from her spanking. Instead we celebrated the victories by squeezing our hands together, her secret audience cheering in silence then swinging quickly down the branches and skipping back to the apartment before she got home and found an empty bed.

Because our father never lived with us in Mombasa, his ghost could not find its way through the narrow and crowded streets, and we were not haunted by the sorrow of his loss.

The weight I carried in my chest was for my mother. She was stoned from the village of her husband, cast out like a witch because she did not die of AIDS like he did and his second and third wives would do. Though strong enough to stand and hurl rocks at us leaving, they too would shrink from their bodies like my father, turning from flesh and blood to bones then dust.

I brought Kembe down from the hills on my back. Mother balanced everything we owned upon her head. No tears. This is something I have inherited from her, too proud to show pain by letting water run from our eyes. How jealous I am of those who can cry. But she had no time to sit and weep, as we only had enough money to ride a truck to the outskirts of Mombasa and find our Uncle.

My mother said her brother was clever, that he had been promoted from a crane operator to the foreman of Mombasa docks. From dawn to dusk he supervised the swinging metal containers, leaving the port loaded with coffee and millet, arriving with everything the world thought Africa needed.

We got to his front door in the dark. Only Kembe had slept in the back of the rattling truck, and I could see my mother was close to collapsing when Uncle Kip opened the door and hugged her to stop her from falling down. He rubbed his knuckles playfully across the top of Kembe's head and told me that I was lucky enough to look like my mother. Then he shook his head and said "Oh Lord, oh Lord" as he listened to how his brother-in-law had receded from the world and widowed his wife and children.

We slept on his living room floor wrapped in a curtain. Uncle Kip woke, dressed and left for the docks before dawn. I asked mother if we had to leave too and she said of course not and told me to go back to sleep. But I lay awake with Kembe and watched the sun hit the windowpane and listened to the volume of the city grow from a quiet chatter to a clattering party of car horns and busses, engines revving and drivers shouting, the daily battle for a Shilling.

When mother woke she cleaned the two-room apartment and told us to shower. Kembe ran the taps until the water crinkled his fingers. It was the first time he had washed without jumping into the river or running to the well with a bucket. In the hills we looked from our glassless window to a vista of rolling hills dotted with trees and wildlife. The new view was a city shaking itself from the dust, standing up against the weight of its inhabitants and the burning sun. Mombasa and the mountains were two different countries.

Uncle Kip spoke to some of his friends at work and got mother a job at the docks. She brewed tea for the men and swept spilt maize and coffee from the wharf. But it was not enough money for us to get our own room or go to school. Kembe and I went with mother to the docks, and while I filled the urn or dried the cups, my little brother played with the sugar cubes, constructing cars and houses, a crude block figure that looked nothing like a man but he called "Father."

Before Uncle Kip lost his shiny smile and grew tired of Kembe sitting on his knee and mother cleaning his little apartment to a polished sheen, he took us to Fort Jesus and bought us bottles of Fanta. We strolled around the sun-washed ramparts, and Uncle Kip slowly read plaques about the Portuguese and the prison.

Outside the walls, beyond the tourists and the security guards, boys younger than Kembe begged for food and money. Uncle Kip threw up his hands and tried to shoo them away. They did not move. They were nearly naked, clutching rags doused with kerosene and holding them under their nostrils. A boy crept to the side of us and snatched the bottle of Fanta from Kembe. He scurried away and Uncle Kip wrapped his arms around us like wings, shielding his niece and nephew from boys who had become more rat than child.

The morning after the night he came home drunk and shouted at my mother because he did not have a wife and never would if he had to play father to the children of his sister, my mother yanked us from the floor and onto the dusty streets. We followed her along to each shop, factory, restaurant and bar, watching her beg for work from the wall or corner she had hidden us behind. The pattern of enquiry and refusal was the same each time. First she adjusted her best headscarf and put her shoulders back, walking upright and proud to the boss with her widest smile and brightest eyes, putting her hands together and pleading for the gift of employment. Then each time she was turned away she somehow lost height, slumping away to the next business without vacancies.

After a day of no food or water, our beaten feet sore of the ground, we headed home through a grey dusk. Mother had not spoken for an hour when she began cursing the spirit of our father, asking the sky what kind of man gave away his wife and children for a single night with another woman.

It would be the kind of man who would pay for our school uniforms, our rent, and the rice in our bowls.

For a while she worked two jobs, in the morning brewing tea at the docks, and in the afternoon cleaning the Paradise. She mopped the floor and washed glasses, wiped down tables and polished the wide mirrors. This money meant we could move to a single room in a house with four other families. Uncle Kip helped us carry our meagre possessions into the new home. He apologised and said he was not throwing us onto the street. My mother said she understood then picked a dead mouse from the floor and flung it through the window.

We chased the mice and cockroaches and played with other children in the house. Mother bought books and a uniform and I went to a new school. I was nearly bottom of my class. Words and letters I had learnt before returned to shapes of silent mystery. Kembe stayed with one of the other families while I studied and mother worked from morning till night.

When Uncle Kip got pneumonia the new foreman gave the sweeping and tea-making job to his cousin. Uncle Kip got better, but was demoted to operating cranes again, and had to move out into a smaller, shared room. Once more mother walked the streets, this time without luck. She still had the Paradise cleaning job, but it was not enough to feed and clothe us, keep a roof over our heads.

We had not eaten the day the landlord came around. He was an old man with a wooden leg. The other families closed their doors when he climbed the narrow staircase to our room. He shuffled from shoe to wooden stump, a tick-tock step that stood the hairs on my neck. When mother said she did not have the money he hit an empty pot across the floor with his crutch. "Time to get some fresh air children." I did not know what he meant. Then mother snapped at me to take Kembe for a walk. We went as far as the front door and listened to his wooden stump tapping out a beat on the floorboards.

After he tick-tocked back down the stairs, after he hobbled from the house, the beads of sweat on his forehead dropping to the road like dirty rain, my mother had a faraway look to her eyes. As though she could see a foreign country at the end of the street.

She got a second job at the Paradise in the evenings. I knew she was not cleaning, but I was too young to understand it was not serving tables either. Every day, on the way home from school, I went to the Paradise and helped her wash the last of the glasses and hang the beer towels on the clothesline before she would go home and change for the night shift. While I polished and dried the counter, she played pool in the empty bar. The electricity was cut during the day, but the bright green baize of the table and the coloured balls glowed with their own soft light. If I spoke to her while she was resting the cue between her thumb and forefinger, taking aim like a marksman, she would not answer. And until the power came back on, and the neon lettering that said Paradise announced the bar was open for business, and the men came and drank as if it were the last river running in Africa, this is where my mother would be.

We moved from the cockroach palace to our own two-bedroom apartment. Kembe started school. After I finished cleaning the bar, while mother practiced and practiced alone, we went to the market and haggled for vegetables and fish, sometimes clothes. Then we would go back to the apartment and I would help mother cook while Kembe did his homework or watched TV with the family next door. These were good times, cooking together like we had done in the hills, a rhythm to the day and place to sleep that was our own. Mother was always happiest when she came back from the bar that night, and not the following morning.

Now I know why. Now I know why she came back to the apartment and beat Kembe for playing with her condoms. One day he found a box of "rubber balloons" in the bottom drawer of her dresser. He unwrapped and inflated every single one until they burst with a pop. Mother screamed, "Do you want me to disappear like your father?" before slapping his face.

When I asked her what she was working as in the evenings she snapped, "What do you care as long as there's food on the table." She mumbled something about being a waitress, that it paid the bills until something better came along.

And something did.

For two nights she played and beat the German. For two nights she did not come home until lunchtime the next day. He was a better player than most, planning three or four shots ahead, his elbow fixed like a hinge for the cue to ride. But he played without flair or adventure, was mechanical and sober and not good enough for my mother.

On the third night Kembe did not wake when I uncurled from the bed and crept from the room. I tiptoed the roofs, walls and broken fences, climbing soundlessly into the mango tree. The bar was almost empty, just the German ordering a drink, my mother chalking her cue and the bored girls smoking and dangling their legs from the high stools. The German carried two drinks back to the table. He walked erect and upright, as if the planet tilted he could be used as a measure to set it level again. He wore silver framed glasses that caught the light, beige trousers and a white shirt.

When he put down the drinks I heard the ice clink against the glass. No music tonight. It was quiet enough for me to hear, and remember, every word.

"We should raise the stakes," said my mother.

She spoke in a tone that scared me. She was inviting him inside her, leaving the made up woman in the mirror of the dresser and talking to him as herself, *My mother.*

"Double or nothing?" suggested the German. "Everything you have won from me, times two. Or zero, the money returned."

"Not enough." My mother stopped twisting the chalk across the tip. She blew the excess dust away with pursed lips. "How about a future?"

The German said nothing and took a cloth from a hook next to the rack then wiped down his cue and rolled the shaft across the table to test if were true.

"A future?"

"A life beyond this."

"In Germany?"

"Yes"

"With me?"

"Yes"

"You are asking for a whole country."

"And a man."

Still my mother did not move. She looked like a little girl. She watched him release the balls through from the workings of the table and arrange them inside the wooden triangle. He then flipped a shilling and caught it on the back of his hand and asked my mother to call heads or tails.

"Tails."

"Tails it is."

Neither of them agreed to the stakes, but when my

mother spread her palm on the baize and broke the pack to start the game, I guessed the bet was on.

I did not understand what I saw, or maybe I did not want to. My mother was sweating like a white man under the lights, the cue shaking in her grip because she was playing for her life. With or without us.

The pack shattered. Balls ricocheted around the table. She had sunk one odd and one even from the break, and now had the choosing of the table. The white was nestled against the remainder of the pack, and my mother straightened her long fingers into a high bridge. She rested her chin on the cue, her forehead glistening.

"You know why this game is so special?" asked the German. He was not watching my mother as he talked. Instead he polished his glasses and brought them to the light to confirm they were spotless.

"No variables," he answered his own question.

My mother played and missed an easy shot.

"No luck. No force acting upon the balls except you or I."

My mother straightened and said she knew this and that was why she loved the game. "No one to blame when things go wrong," she added.

"Exactly," announced the German. "Life has other people, variables we do not and cannot control. This game is pure, each time we pick up the cue with have absolute control over our own destiny. What a rare moment."

Now the German took the table. He seemed to move more fluidly than the previous evenings. First he slotted an easy ball into the corner pocket, but with such a whiplash of his wrist that the spinning white accelerated up the table and slowed to rest in line for a lone even, snug against the back cushion. After he cut this ball into the corner he potted four more without lifting his head. The crack, drop, and clunk of the ball rolling through the workings of the table was usually the winning beat and rhythm of my mother. Tonight she was standing and listening to someone else.

"Mathematics," said the German. "Angles and numbers, degrees of force." He doubled a ball into the middle pocket. "*Scheisse.*" He had not brought the white far enough up the table to leave a line on his remaining even. "Perfect sums, flawed humans." He bounced the white off the back cushion to bring it back and glance his final ball, saving the two shots but leaving my mother with an open table.

She walked a circuit, slowly, maybe planning every shot until the end of the game before she crouched and set her stance, the cue an extension of her body. She drilled each ball from the table, definite and sure of success. The German stood and did not speak. But this time he watched every shot, consumed by my mother. She potted six consecutive balls, leaving only the black and the last even on the baize. For the first time she looked up from the table, at the German finishing his drink, looking into the empty glass as though he could divine the future, then smiling, because he needed no reading of what was going to happen.

"Is the bet still on?" asked my mother. He nodded. Then she crouched to the table and named the corner pocket. She did not miss. She fired the black from the table with such force that the girls at the bar looked over to see what sound had disturbed the quiet night.

Then the German put down his empty glass and walked around the table and took the cue from my mother and placed it in the rack.

Next he took her hand in his.

***

Once a week, and only if there have been no complaints from the guests about housekeeping, the management give a stale Black Forest gateau to the staff as a bonus. For a cleaner to buy a single slice from the restaurant they would have to work for five hours. But at least the cream would be fresh, and the glaze on the cherries still shining.

Stale or not, Mercy has acquired a taste for expensive German cakes and peels away the foil and cuts herself a slice. She does not ask the Russians at the table if they want any because she already knows the answer.

"This what I did on the farm," says Anna, one of the Ukrainian chambermaids. "Throwing the bad food to the pigs." Anna was a lecturer in Classic Russian Literature at the University of Odessa until her daughter was diagnosed with leukaemia. Cleaning toilets in a German Hotel pays four times the hourly rate of deconstructing The Idiot. And Euros convert into chemotherapy much more readily than the Hryvnia.

Mercy cuts and ignores her. She likes Anna, she knows why she is here, the sacrifice from mother to child. But she needs to keep a professional distance as she hopes the next cleaner to be promoted to Head Housekeeper will be her. Though only if the manager does not discover that she can barely read or write.

"Do they think we are living in the pigsty?" Every day Anna simmers with anger while she strips beds and picks up dirty clothes. German teenagers order her to shine taps and unblock hair from plugholes. This is her moment of protest. "Really, it encourages them to treat us this way."

Mercy lifts the slice onto her plate and sits down.

The other Ukrainians leave the cake because Anna told them too. Mercy takes a large bite, leaving cream smeared on her top lip that she wipes off with a hotel napkin.

"*You should have more pride, Mercy.*"

Serge, an undergraduate from Kiev who vacuums hallways and scrubs toilets to save for his MA, sharply scolds Anna in Russian.

But it is too late. Mercy carefully sets the cake down on the plate. Anna may have blonde hair and blue eyes, but Mercy does not see the two of them as so different. "Pride, you say?" She screws up the napkin in her fist. "I have slept with men for a bowl of rice."

No one talks or eats. No one looks her in the eye except Anna.

"*And my children ate every single grain, glad to have some food in their stomachs.*"

Mercy reaches out across the table and grabs the knife. Anna shudders. But Mercy only leans to cut another slice of gateau. She then puts down the knife and takes a fresh napkin from the dispenser and lays it out on the table. She wraps both pieces of cake in the monogrammed tissue and tucks them away deep in her apron pocket.

"*I'm sorry, Mercy.*"

Mercy stands and tells Anna not to worry. She tells her that she is right, and that she lost the meaning of pride the day she boarded a plane to Germany.

She will eat the gateau on her break. She used to sneak off from her duties and take naps in the vacant rooms. She used to treat herself to the individually wrapped cookies and watch Internet TV with her shoes off and feet up on the crisp white sheets. If she wants to be promoted she has to set a good example, but today is an exception because it is the opening ceremony of the 2012 Olympics.

Sport is not her only love, her distraction from the past. One of her favourite shows is the soap where the audience votes on the storyline, the fate of the characters. Viewers press a button on their remote controls to decide whether a bored housewife has an affair, if a father should be told the child is not his, whether a young couple elope or stay.

This was the most control she ever had over the direction of a life, including her own.

Though she would not admit this to any of the other foreign staff, the Ukrainians, the Indonesians, the Chinese and the other Africans, she had a morbid fascination for the British show, Let me in, I'm an Asylum Seeker!

Since the reinforcement of the EU Refugee Charter and the rapidly expanding dustbowl of the Sahara, migrants had been flocking into Europe. In desperate efforts to halt the flow, Spain had ceded sovereignty of the Canary Islands and its Moroccan enclaves so African refugees could no longer use the extended territories as stepping-stones into Europe. Italy had begun construction of a floating "Security Boom," a 300-kilometre fence bobbing just outside their southern sea border, ensuring boats of refugees from Libya were intercepted before the finish line of a shot at EU citizenship.

The show, despite protests from Human Rights groups, was popular because each week, from almost anywhere in the developing world, twelve men and women competed for a single, genuine, maroon passport.

Challenges included "The Spelling Scramble," where all the contestants were asked to spell out a word with a limited number of oversized letters. Mercy would clap out loud when the women pulled vowels and consonants from the hands of the men, correctly spelling bonus words like "Democracy" and "Parliament" to make it through to the next round. The job interview and Royal history quiz were followed by her favourite challenge, "The Dinner Party."

Here, the surviving four asylum seekers had to demonstrate impeccable manners and correct decorum at the dining table. First points were won and lost choosing a gift. From bumper bags of crisps to vintage bottles of wine, the opening faux pas would be made on the doorstep. The right or wrong present was followed by incorrect greetings, camera close ups of wet fish handshakes, and kisses actually making contact with cheeks.

But the real tension was at the table, an arena of etiquette waiting to be broken. No contestant had ever scored maximum points, and each week acts of fatal rudeness, deliberate or not, would be penalised with disqualification. Slurping soup, eating with hands, dipping bread, refusing seconds and forgetting to over compliment the host whether the food was delicious or not, were grounds for instant dismissal. When the "Rudeometer" buzzed, the chair slid back and tipped the asylum seeker into a tube. The camera then magically panned to the contestant appearing from the supposed end of the shoot at Felixstowe Holding Centre.

Mercy still chuckles when she thinks of the Congolese man who plucked a handful of boiled potatoes from the serving dish and burnt his fingertips. He threw them across the table as if they had jumped alive from his grip.

She can laugh without guilt or cruelty because she believes the man has a better chance of happiness in the country of his birth. Whether or not it is ravaged by civil war, drought, corruption, disease, occupation, dictatorship, or famine.

But this is the thought of a woman who lost her children to Africa like dust on the wind.

She loved her son and daughter, not the second man she had sworn to partner until the end of his or her days. She had crookedly signed her name on a form she could not read in a draughty Berlin registry office. She signed it in the hope a piece of paper would one day secure the future for her son and daughter, that they would understand their mother when she lifted them from the slums of Mombasa and into a life where she would not live in fear of them being orphaned by a burst condom.

He did not know she had a son and daughter waiting and praying for her to walk back through the door she had closed on them.

He had not even kissed her in Kenya, but after a blood test in a spotless clinic overlooking a lake of ducks and geese, he had sex with her every night. But it was not her he thrashed and sweated against. Her body had long ago learnt to exist separately from her soul, performing automatically, convincing an aging man he was once again a virile and acrobatic youth doling electric pleasures. He was in fact a divorcee popping Viagra and countering a midlife crisis by flying back from Africa with a bride half his age. And a black bride in a very white town, stared at as though she had stepped onto their cobbled streets from another planet.

He was not a bad man, but he was not a "man" either, not as Mercy would measure a husband, anyway. He had no children from his previous marriage, and seemed to have devoted what Mercy could find of his heart and soul to his collection of classic cars. His successful accountancy firm meant he could hire a cleaner and gardener. Mercy had nothing to do but watch TV and pray for her children, talk to the Filipino housekeeper who mopped an already gleaming floor.

Mercy was waiting for her passport, counting down the days, and slowly accumulating his money. She took one note a day from his wallet. She took two or three coins from the change in his pocket. Mercy feared if anyone would notice the missing weight in their trousers it would be an accountant, and swapped higher denominations for lower ones, changing the amount, but keeping the number of coins the same. When she walked into the pretty little town and bought vegetables and meat, a quarter of the change was put into an empty coffee jar, which she kept buried at the bottom of a large pot of rice.

Six months later, two days after a courier arrived at the door and she had signed a cross for her passport with trembling fingers, she waited for the hum of his car engine to diminish into the pine trees before packing her bags, emptying the coffee jar and catching a bus to the station. From their she took a train to the airport, a plane to Mombasa, and finally a taxi to her flat, where the door was opened by a child not hers.

***

My father was born at the height of clouds. He entered the world wailing, lungs pumping the mountain air and desperate for oxygen. He lived because he had the breath of a Kalenjin, as had his father and his grandfather before, a long line of proud and noble descendants from the ancient tribe of highlanders from the hills of the Great Rift Valley.

He grew up at an altitude where visiting relatives from the lowlands fainted and had to sit and take a rest from the sky. A village where the rhythm of life was set by the stars and the moon, the sun and the rain, a village where horseless cowboys herded the cattle, and my father and his brothers ran down the strays barefoot.

Like all Kalenjin boys he ran everywhere. He ran to school. He ran home from school. He ran to gather firewood. He ran to the river to fetch water and spilt none running back. He ran but did not race. Running was not a sport. It was a way of life. A man with more cattle could afford more women and children. My mother was the first of his three wives. I was his seventh and final son.

Before he got sick, before my mother walked my sister and I down from the hills with all our possessions balanced upon her head, he financed his family through the Kalenjin tradition of cattle rustling.

He and his brother would wake in the glow of

dawn, eat a bowl of rice and drink a cup of steaming tea, warming their bodies and working their leg muscles by the heat of a fire tended by my mother. Then they would stand and stretch and run into the rising sun for two days out and three days in, a round trip of a hundred miles or more. And not slower on the return because they were tired, but because they had to drive the wayward cattle up the steep slopes, their lowland lungs heaving in the thinning air, hooves run ragged on the paths of volcanic stone, urged on by the call and whistle of my father.

I have a memory of riding his shoulders up the hillside, the swinging bells hung around the necks of the cattle tinkling, the herd guided along by the sound of his beautiful singing, back to the village he was born in, back to the village he would die in. *Home,* a word no matter how hard or fast I run toward I get no closer.

Maybe this was why the Reverend Thomas Orphanage was no place to rest.

We found Germany in an atlas donated by the Lions Club of Sydney. You could actually walk there from Kenya. With a ruler I drew the most direct route possible from Mombasa to Berlin. North into Ethiopia, Sudan and Egypt, turning right over the Suez Canal and following the Mediterranean coast along Palestine, Israel, Lebanon, Syria and Turkey, before heading inland and crossing from Asia to Europe and walking in a north-western line through Bulgaria, Romania, Hungary, the Slovak and Czech Republic, finally crossing the border into Germany near the south-western tip of Poland.

I was nine years old and small for my age, but I was big enough to know the journey was pure fantasy. I had heard stories of refugees from The Congo and Sudan walking all the way to the shores of the Indian Ocean, but never of two children barefoot to Europe.

The one postcard that made it to the apartment pictured a golden angel hovering over a city of steel and stone. The back of the card was blank. Mother could not read or write, and someone else must have copied out the address for her. I guess she was too embarrassed to ask them to write *Missing you* or *Home soon*.

The day the Dortmund Latter Day Saints hefted four boxes of bibles and two pallet loads of exercise books from their coach, I patiently queued up with a hundred other orphans. I was given another bible, another exercise book, and a blank postcard like the one my mother had already sent.

After we had performed for the camera flashes of our visitors, after I had sung hymns and danced to *Jambo Bwana,* I grabbed at their dangling bags. I clung to legs and tugged at clothes. I asked every single one of the visitors if they had been to Berlin, if they had seen the golden angel, if they had seen my mother.

Most just patted my head and creased the corners of their eyes when they smiled. One woman wore gloves and was afraid of me touching her. Another woman said Berlin was a very big city and a long way from Kenya. She squatted down and reached into her backpack and pulled out a red lollipop. She did the smile thing with the corners of her eyes and placed the lollipop in my hand. I gave it her back. "She's near the golden angel," I said.

"Well," she said sharply. "Did she get on a plane? Because I tell you now, she didn't walk there." She offered the lollipop again and this time I took it. "I'll keep my eyes open for her," she promised.

I ran outside. Lana was already there, picking up stones and throwing them angrily into the bush. "I hate Germans," she said.

If the woman who gave me the lollipop did see my mother, she never came back to tell me.

We lived in the orphanage because we had no parents. We had no parents because my father was buried in the hills and my mother had gone out and never come back. She had hugged and kissed my face and said she had to go away for a while. She promised she would be back soon and that when she returned I would never go hungry again. My cheeks were wet from her tears. When she tried to kiss and hug Lana goodbye my sister kicked and begged her not to leave. For the last time my mother locked the door and left Lana wailing on the floor. She lay there curled and sobbing until Uncle Kip arrived and dropped down his suitcase.

We waited for our mother to come home, but she did not. Uncle Kip either worked or drank. He laughed a lot and wrestled with me, but he did not cook rice very well or pick us up from school. He said mother had gone away for us, her children, that she would be back soon with a bag filled with toys and clothes.

It seemed as though one day Uncle Kip was laughing and joking, and the next he had pneumonia, again. Lana put wet towels on his head and made him cups of black tea. He kept saying he would be well soon, that he was just preparing for our next wrestling bout. He told us to take money from his wallet and send for his doctor. We gave the money to an Indian man at the hospital who thumbed through a draw of files. He pulled out a worn, brown folder and shook his head. He asked if Mr Lotuna was our father. Lana explained he was our Uncle and looking after us while our mother was away. Then the doctor returned the file to the draw and gave us back the money.

Lana had nursed father to the end the same way. The morning we found Uncle Kip staring at the ceiling, she just closed his eyelids and pulled the sheet over his face as though she had been performing the last rites on dying men her whole life.

His friends from the docks clubbed together and gave us some money and said they would call round soon and check we were OK. They did not, and the rent ran out. We left before the landlord came round and negotiated the tenancy with Lana like the one legged man from the cockroach palace.

We became the rat children we had been afraid of when we had food, a roof over our heads, a mother. We slept in doorways, on rocks by the sea, under trees and trucks. We slept on waste ground where people dumped the bodies of babies. I thought they were lost dolls until I smelt their death. The food and clothes we fled the flat with dissolved into the very streets we had to tread. Older boys ripped the shoes from my feet. When stallholders at the market saw us lingering they picked up stones and cocked their arms back like cata-pults. We rummaged with goats and crows in the garbage piles at the back of restaurants. We mugged foreign tourists with other street children, shredding a ladies handbag, scrabbling in the gutter for torn dollars and broken makeup. We begged for food outside the roped off tables of outdoor cafes, competing for a meal with the bare boned dogs. The police chased us for sport. The police chased us when a politician was un-popular and ordered a clean up of the streets. The

Police shot a boy dead who was sleeping on the roof of the Nat West bank. The police arrested the older girls and took them to the cells and only released them after sex.

If I had a thought in my head during this time on the street I do not remember. Instinct kept us alive, the animal will that knew where the Nuns would be handing out bread, which tourist would spare a coin, what patch of pavement would be a bed for a night, a safe space till morning, and not haunted by the men who stalked the shadows, hungry for the child who had no one to call for help.

The stories we passed around were nightmares come true. Vanishings, beatings, dead children floating in the bay. When I slept Lana did not. When she closed her eyes I clutched a rusty screwdriver and waited for the sun. Each day was lifetime, a mission from one meal to the next. I cannot say how long we could have lived like this, as every morning was a miracle. But when a minibus pulled up with THE REVEREND THOMAS ORPHANAGE printed on the side in big blue letters, and two women got out with smiles as bright and wide as my mother, it was as though we had been offered a hand up from hell.

Of the eleven children in the minibus, picked up from the pavement like piles of dirty rags, only four of us could stay at this orphanage. After a nurse had pricked our arms with needles and left us to play in a room with cuddly toys and colouring books, some of the children had to get into the minibus again and go to another orphanage where they did not usually leave.

But our life returned, or least part of it, the busy but empty days flashing past. We collected eggs, milked the cows, shovelled out the pigsty and ran to class. Lana played football with the older boys at break time. She thumped the beaten up ball across that dusty pitch as though it were something she were trying to kill. She was already taking the shape of a woman as powerful and tall as our mother. I watched her slide tackle the boys, brush the dirt from her dress and play on. My fearless sister.

One game she cut her foot on the drain cover that jutted from the centre circle. She limped off and pushed away the other girls when they tried to help her. I sprinted to the tap and filled a bottle of water to wash out her gashed instep. Blood dripped onto the dirt. I cleaned the wound and she sucked air sharply between her teeth. She never cried. I tore a strip of material from my trousers and together we bandaged her foot.

She had only cut herself and I was terrified she was going to vanish, like my mother.

"Whatever happens," she said, looking at me and knowing what bedwetting dreams of abandonment haunted the dormitory at night. "I'll never leave you, never. We're all we have. We must take care of each other. You understand, Kembe."

I said I did. I said that was why we must go to Germany and find mother, together. "Are we going to run or walk?" she mocked. "Maybe grow wings and fly?" She shook her head and tutted. Then she tried not listening but I told her anyway. I told her that soon she would be too old to live in the orphanage, and that she would have to work at the Paradise like mother, and that she too would disappear into the night.

Then she hit me. Not hard, but enough to punish my words, the insult. I had compared her to the woman in the bar, the mother who had flown the nest and left her young to fend for themselves. I bit my lip, gritted my teeth and felt my eyes swell. We sat in silence, watching the other girls and boys playing football.

And when a plane angled into the sky above Mombasa, when the wings flashed with sun as it banked north and rose higher than the mountains our father was buried, we understood there was a way we could ascend this patch of dusty earth.

A month later, her foot healed but still bandaged, Lana was climbing over the security fence at Mombasa Airport. It was nearly dawn. She was profiled against the paling blue sky, perched over the barbed wire scanning the runway for soldiers and dogs. "Now, Kembe."

I scrambled up the mesh fence, higher than the wooden gate at the orphanage we had gone over the night before. I carried our supplies in a plastic bag. We had one bottle of water each, a green banana, a pack of biscuits and a coat I had stolen from an unlocked taxi at the docks. This had been the first stop of the escape, where we waited out the heat and searchlight of day in an empty shipping container. When darkness came we had slipped from shadow to shadow, invisible, already wise to what danger the streets held, what lurked in the men with drink, the men in uniform.

Lana dropped down from the fence and cursed when she landed on her bad foot. We had walked the highway all night to make the airport before sunrise, and her cut had opened up again, staining the dirty bandage red. "Hurry, Kembe."

I was straddled over the top of the fence. We had folded and wadded the coat over the barbs so we would not be snagged and discovered in the morning like washing hung out to dry. I swung my legs onto the runway side and tugged at the coat, twanging wire along the length of the fence. Lana was crouched on the grass, "Leave it." I could see a luggage cart trundling from a hangar towards us. I pulled at the coat again. "What are you fooling around at?"

But we needed the coat, I was sure of that much. Planes flew higher than the peak of Mount Kenya, and there was snow on her all year round. Closer to the sun or not, it would be cold above the clouds.

"Kembe," Lana hissed. The headlight of the luggage cart was getting brighter. I pulled my feet from the holes in the mesh and swung on the sleeve of the coat. It tore like paper and I fell as the cart rattled past.

We lay flat in the grass. We watched a plane taxi from the terminal along the tarmac to the edge of the runway. It waited for another plane that swooped from the sky like a great white bird. Air roared through the turbines. The landing gear lowered from the undercarriage like dangled talons. When the wheels touched down puffs of burnt rubber appeared then vanished, and the weight and power that had somehow defied gravity made earth again.

We crept closer to the terminal. We watched other Kenyans board planes with propellers, not jet engines, not the propulsion required to rocket us to another continent. The only jet that white people boarded did not stop at the runway junction, thundering straight into the cloudless blue, the engines as loud in our chests as our beating hearts.

Lana and I had been hidden in the grass for two hours, ready to run hand in hand for our lift to the sky, when a sleek white jet purred from a hangar separate to the main terminal. Lana asked me if I knew what the

German flag looked like. I was angry I did not. I knew the shape of its land, the names of the countries that surrounded its borders, how it had almost no coast.

"Red, white, and blue. Think Kembe."

"Yes," I said. "It was on the food cartons that came by ship. The vitamin biscuits that tasted of sawdust."

"From Germany?"

I had no chance to say yes or no. The jet had stopped. Lana took my hand and ran. I could not feel the tarmac beneath my feet. It felt as though we were already flying, rushing into space.

The noise roared beyond something called sound, juddering the bones in our body, the very air we breathed. We ducked as we ran because we thought the clouds were crashing from the sky. Lana was shouting something, maybe "The wheels." The supersonic whir drowned out the entire world.

I followed Lana beneath the wings. She sprang from the hub to the tread, and then turned to offer her hand and haul us both into the compartment above. We clung to loose pipes, wedged our feet onto lips of metal. We braced ourselves for take off. The engine whined and screamed. My teeth chattered in my skull. Lana had a fistful of my shirt, and I could not fall out if I tried. When I shouted "The coat," I did not even hear the words myself. I hoped I was wrong about the cold.

We did not make it to Germany. We never even left Kenya. When the screaming engines slowed, idled, then actually stopped, my ears rang with silence. After all that sound the quiet seemed like the death of God.

We waited, trembling and mute. We heard movement inside the plane, a door opening, soldiers speaking Swahili then English, boots on tarmac. We froze to where we had fastened ourselves, thinking will power alone could camouflage us against the steel undercarriage.

Even when three scruffy soldiers and a foreigner in a suit craned their necks and stared into our eyes we did not, or could not, move. I had been holding on so tight my hand was a claw. Pointed guns meant nothing. Only when they reached up and pulled Lana down by her ankle did I let go.

Now we were afraid. The foreigner watched while the guards plucked us from the runway like dolls of straw. I shrugged and struggled, wriggled to yank myself free. The guard who was holding neither of us slapped me hard across the back of my head. "Don't be so ungrateful, boy," he said. "We just saved your stupid lives."

They all smelt of alcohol. Their uniforms were dirty and not properly buttoned. The guard who had just hit me watched my sister as though she were walking across the dance floor in the Paradise.

I wished I were bigger and stronger.

I wished my father were alive.

We were too afraid to speak to each other. Or I was too afraid to speak to Lana, defiant every step, forcing the guard to push her along with the butt of his rifle. Only when we had been frogmarched into a falling down outhouse and along a corridor stale with mouse droppings and stagnant water did I see fear on her face for the first time in my life.

The two guards shoved us into a dank room with a single window. The glass was crisscrossed with mesh. A wooden chair with a broken leg lay toppled on its side. The concrete floor was stained with oil. The guard in charge with a red hat and missing teeth ordered away his juniors.

I stood with Lana in the corner. No way out but through this boar of a man. He filled the doorframe. He stood watching his men leave. We heard another door slam and then he turned into the room. He looked only at my only sister. He smiled. He said he would teach her a lesson she would not forget. He walked toward her, the gap between his teeth a black hole that would devour us both. Then he was close enough to stand before her, over her. He smelt of rum, sweat and shit. He was too fat to do up the top button of his trousers. He reached out for Lana and she slapped his hand away and screamed that she would tell the police. He threw his head back and laughed then grabbed her by the throat and shunted her against the wall.

I bit his arm like a crocodile.

He screamed like a pig.

Lana picked up the wooden chair and smashed it down on the bridge of his nose. It opened up a red dent. He growled. My jaw was fastened and I tasted blood. He punched the back of my head. The second time he hit me the air turned black.

I want to say that I got up and crushed his skull in my bare hands. I want to say that I wrung his neck and watched his life wriggle and gasp away.

I cannot.

It was the foreign man from the plane who walked into the room and saved my sister. He looked at Lana on the floor, her torn dress. He looked at the officer unbuckling his belt then stepped toward him and swatted him against the wall. The officer twitched on the floor and bled, another tooth missing from his grimace.

Why the foreign man came to that room at the

moment I do not know. We did not wait for explanations. We bolted from the room, along the corridor and into the light, flashing past the guards leant against an oil drum smoking, too slow to catch us running for our lives. Before they had even stubbed out their cigarettes and put their guns to their shoulders we were gone, behind the crumbling office, over a pile of plane tyres and back to the other side of the fence.

On our stomachs again, we crawled through the long grass and waited, daring no more than a whisper, ready to spring once more if they came hacking through the bushes with machetes and dogs.

I was shivering with fear. I wanted to cry, but Lana held my hand when she was not on her haunches keeping look out, ready to fight or fly again.

"They won't come," she said and shook her head. "Cowards." She spat. "I wish it were me who'd knocked that pig to ground."

Between the boom of planes taking off and landing, the roar and the quiet, we listened to life in the shacks and slums that clung to the jet-shuddered earth surrounding the runway. These tin huts were the homes of lucky children, those who did not wander the motherless streets as naked as a foal on the savannah, every hungry hyena and lion drawn to the scent of easy prey.

Beyond the gates of the orphanage there was nothing. Lana could only stay another month. When a girl or boy reached their sixteenth birthday they had to leave. They had to pack their bags and face the city alone because other children living in the gutter were waiting for their bed.

Each time a sixteenth birthday came around, there was an excited shuffle of possessions in the dormitory.

The older you were, the better position of your bed. Youngest by the stinking toilets, eldest by a window with a mosquito screen. We scrambled from bed to bed without realising the closer we got to fresh air, the closer we got to exit day.

Lana slept by a screen window that she could slide back to watch the moonrise over the trees. She let me sit on her bed after lights out. She told me stories about the animals of the plains, the mighty elephants and fierce cats, hippos wallowing in the mud, gazelles as quick as light. I asked her where animals went when they died, if they went to the same heaven as our father. "Of course," she said. "Well, just the good animals. And when the hunters and poachers have been busy, and heaven is overflowing with hyenas and wildebeest, monkeys and lions, God lets them graze the surface of the moon. Look carefully and you can see the black and white hide of the zebras. On a quiet night, when the whole of Africa is fast asleep, you can hear the trumpet of an elephant calling across space."

I used to dream that a giraffe would lean through the window of the dormitory and wake me from sleep. She would lower her head so I could climb onto her back. I would ride her soundlessly across the savannah, kicking up silver dust in the starlight, swaying to and fro with each graceful stride before she stepped into the sky and carried me to the moon. These were beautiful dreams, gliding in to a herd of elephants lifting their trunks, a fanfare of arrival from my father, astride the head of the herd and beaming at his son, King of Kings on top of the moon.

When the sun dipped below the horizon and tinged the indigo sky pink, a woman with a baby strapped across her back collecting firewood almost discovered us hiding in the grass. Lana clutched my arm and told me she was not going back.

"Neither am I," I swore.

I crawled after my sister to the fence. I followed the bloodied bandage of her wounded foot. We scrabbled to the edge of the tall grass, to where it had been hacked to its roots to clear a line of sight for the guards. Before we had just climbed over. This time we waited, in the knowledge we were prey.

Only when the earth turned us far enough from the sun to dissolve our shadows into dusk, did we jump the fence. With no coat to wad the barbs, we both fell to the grass with cuts and scratches on our hands and feet.

"The coat and bag," I said. "The water."

We ran stooped, close to the ground, scurrying towards the terminal, to where the coat and bag still lay. We splashed the water on our cuts and gulped down the rest. "Enjoy it Kembe," said Lana, smiling. "This is the last drop of Kenyan water you'll ever drink."

The next plane that taxied to the edge of the runway had a red, white, and blue flag on its tailfin. "The same colours, but different," said Lana.

The warning lights pulsed. The engines howled. Through the porthole windows we could see white people doing up their seatbelts and reading magazines. We both saw the same boy playing with a wooden giraffe.

"Now."

We ran hand in hand. I had the coat tied around my waist. The plane was gigantic, two engines on each wing, two floors of windows. It seemed a machine too huge to float us above the clouds.

Just as we made it beneath the wing, the turbines

whined at a higher pitch, and the plane began to taxi onto the runway, all that bulk unstoppable until it landed in another country. We sprinted beneath the undercarriage to the front, Lana tugging me behind. The huge wheel was turning slowly enough for me to stand on a rivet and use the revolution as a lift onto the landing gear arm. I turned and held out my hand for Lana. She tried the same trick, but the plane was moving faster now, and the turning wheel flipped her head over heels onto the tarmac. I yelled her name as loud as the engine screamed. She picked herself up and sprinted. But as she gathered speed, so did the plane. The warning lights pulsed. Lana flickered in and out of the darkness. In the dazzle between each illumination I was blinded. I thought each flash of her face was the last, my final picture. One moment she was touching my outstretched fingers, the next she was stumbling beyond my reach, falling further back from the accelerating plane.

But I held out my hand. I reached into the dark until she clutched through the noise and terror and I hauled her onboard. We climbed the landing gear into the stowage compartment. Again we wedged ourselves in, jamming our feet between pipes and tubes. Lana gripped my shirt as though she were tearing it from my back. The white lines of the runway became one, the tarmac a blur.

Then we were flying, leaving earth. We were angling into the sky toward my mother, to where the moon and stars hung in heaven, where giraffes cantered across space and my father lived like a King upon the back an elephant.

And before the wheels folded us into the belly of the plane, before the doors sealed our fate to the thin and frozen air, for the second time we climbed higher than the shadow of Africa, chasing down the embers of a day, blessed once more by the setting sun.

***

Mercy pushes a cart of cleaning equipment through the lobby, past a tour group of British guests impatiently waiting to check in. The voice recognition software has again failed to register the conso-nants of the Polish receptionist. He is repeating the name "Grewcock" at the monitor. Nothing is happening. He continues to repeat the name of the family of four from Bedford. He sounds like an old CD, stalled on a minute scratch. The teenage children lean over the walnut counter to try and look at the screen. The girl shouts "Grewcock" and her father pulls her down. The screen is still blank, and the receptionist has no keys to prod in anger and throws his hands into the air and calls the bellboy to fetch the manager.

Mercy shuffles past and tries to make herself invisible from the kerfuffle. She does not want to be delayed. She is on duty in the lounge again, a favour from the Head Housekeeper so she can watch the Olympics while she empties ashtrays and clears glasses.

After the razzamatazz of the opening ceremony, the fire-works and lasers, dancers and singers, the flag waving teams beamed to the billions, Mercy watched every race the Kenyans entered. Seeing the athletes parade around the stadium in the black, red and green of her homeland, she had quietly wept while she wiped down tables. When the Bar Manager asked what was wrong she told him it was the ammonia in the cleaning fluid that had made her eyes water. It was the first time she had cried in seven years.

Again, Mercy took to sneaking into the vacant rooms during her shifts away from the Lounge. She watched, clapped and cheered when her fellow countrymen and women raced. The men reminded her of her husband, striking out at dawn to bring back cattle, watching his silhouette extinguished by the rising sun.

Augustine Choge took gold in the 3,000m and 5,000m, but it was Marathon runner Lucy Wangui, collapsing on the rain drenched streets within sight of the finish line, that had Mercy singing out prayers for the first time since she had set foot in Africa, since she had found that her family had gone as though they had never even been.

After strangers opened the door to the flat she had left her children and brother, she hurried to the docks to find out where they were, what had happened. The new foreman took off his hard hat to speak to Mercy and she knew then that her brother was dead. "The children," she screamed, "What about my little boy and girl." The new foreman did not know. Mercy went back to the apartment block and banged on the door of the neighbours. Different families had moved in and out, but the family from Nairobi who used to let Kembe sit and watch TV opened the door. The wife cried and said she barely had enough to feed her own children and could not take two more. "Where did you go?" she asked Mercy. "Why did you leave them?"

Mercy walked the streets in search of her children. The destitute boys and girls who made the pavement their home could now be her son and daughter.

But she did not find them. She asked at the market, at the school, and even at the Paradise where the other girls looked at her new shoes and leather handbag as though she were the peak of achievement and success. Outside she pulled off her heels and paced the streets, the alleys and the waste ground. She checked the orphanages and none of the hundreds of parentless children were hers. At the Reverend Thomas Orphanage the director told her that two children had runaway only week ago. She was not sure if they were hers. When Mercy saw the love and care the volunteers showered on their children, she wondered if she was worthy of motherhood anyway.

Kenya had become as empty as Germany. She would go back to a country where she would fail to forget a life she had ruined. But not to him, her sham of a husband. With the return half of her ticket she took the plane back to Berlin and answered an ad for a cleaner in a Bavarian hotel.

Seven years on she is in the lounge of a four star hotel clearing tables and trying not to get between the guests and the CineSon. Hard work makes her happy, frees her mind from the past. It is the 800m final, and both a German and British athlete is in the line up. The room is crowded with face-painted children waving flags, the flash bang crosses of the Union Jack, the burnt depth of the black, red and yellow of Germany.

The race is close. The British runner leads until the last hundred metres, flailing his arms like a bird at the tape to try and thrust his body beyond the advancing German. The finish is too close to call. Guests cheer and jeer and crowd the screen to plead with the judges to declare their runner the winner. The first photo shows a dead heat, but when the camera zooms in, it is undoubtedly the triumphant chest of the German that has crossed the line first. Even the stern restaurant manager from Munich jumps into the air when the result is confirmed. The volume of the German guests celebrations is as powerful as the silence of the British.

"He cheated," bellows a drunken Mr Ashcroft from Bude, briefly threatening joviality and the Olympic spirit. His teenage daughters shrink into their chairs. "You can see the engine under his vest." He staggers, sloshes beer from a Steiner onto his wife. "BMW in his pants."

The Germans laugh. This is a compliment. The girls plead "Dad!" and he flops down. Mercy gets a cloth and wipes the table and passes Mrs Ashcroft a tissue.

"You're not bloody German," blurts Mr Ashcroft, slouched in the chair, his ruddy face topped with a nose as bright as a strawberry.

"*John!*" *snaps his wife.*

Mercy has heard far worse than this. "*Once upon a time I was from Kenya, but my passport is German now.*"

"*We're all bloody related anyway.*"

An embarrassed Mrs Ashcroft has her nails dug into her palms, but her husband continues.

"*Well, we all stood up and walked out of Africa.*"

Mercy takes his glass. "*But some more recently than others, and some whether they wanted to or not.*"

She moves on to wipe down the next table and Mr Ashcroft shouts after her. "*Like our little man in the steeplechase. Born in Kenya, but all roast beef and Yorkshire pudding now.*"

Mercy does not listen. He is drunk. She takes the empties from the table and stacks them into each other then turns the ashtray upside down into the waste bag. She may as well be invisible, weaving between the holidaymakers, reaching around conversations and elbows for glasses. When the tray is full she zigzags back to the bar, lifts up the hatch and steps behind the counter. Four glasses at a time, she stacks the dishwasher, closes the door then turns it on. Beyond the kitchen she can hear people booing, the British guests heckling. No German has reached the final of the steeplechase, and in an attempt to change the commentary from German to English, the restaurant manager has crashed the CineSon into a jumble of pixels.

"*Here,*" *Mercy takes the remote from his hand and deftly flicks from the scrambled picture to the language selection menu. She is cheered and applauded when the sound of an excited, almost breathless, English commentator fills the room.*

"And they're off! The 2012 Steeplechase final is underway. And what expectations we have for the young Britain, Njenga. We knew he had talent after the fantastic times he clocked at the European Championships. We knew that he was capable of competing with the best in his field, but to be here, before the glittering flashbulbs of the Olympic Stadium, a crowd roaring his name already as the pack, jostling for position at the first hurdle begins to open up, with the Ethiopian, as expected, setting an electrifying pace."

Mercy speaks English better than she does German, but she has not heard or seen any of the race yet, as again she is on her hands and knees, soaking up a puddle of spilt red wine and carefully picking up shards of broken glass from beneath the table of Mr and Mrs Ashcroft. When she lifts her head to wring out the cloth, Mr Ashcroft shouts, "This one, this one." He is flapping his arms and pointing wildly. "Young Mjembe, or whatever his name his."

Mercy gets onto one knee and turns her head to the screen, the bobbing heads of the athletes. When she sees an African man in a British vest, running in the style of her dead husband rounding up stray cattle, she stands and walks up to screen until she is close enough to reach out and touch it.

"Clear over the hurdle and into the water, splashing from the pool with consummate balance. Have you ever seen the face of runner so determined? Sixth place and approaching the penultimate lap, some way off from the leader and the following group, but we know he can finish, that he has gas in the tank for the last lap."

"Who is he?" Mercy asks the screen. But the commentator is talking about other runners and she turns to the German guests closest to the action. "Wer ist er?" They shake their heads. "Wo-her kommt er?" They do not know and they shirk back at the force of her questioning. Mercy looks back to the race. "Lord, Lord, say his name."

..

"We all know his incredible story. We all know he runs with nine toes and not ten. That frostbite took his little toe on the journey here, tied to the undercarriage of a 747 by a ragged coat, only surviving the cold because of a ruptured pipe leaking air from the cabin. And off he goes! Kembe Njenga, accelerating beyond the trailing pack. He was told he was too small to run the steeplechase, but here he is, skipping hurdles on the penultimate lap of the 2012 final, bounding towards the finish line. Come on Kembe!"

Mercy watches him run, the Kenyan in red, white and blue. Did the commentator really say the name of her son? She does not believe him. She does not believe what she can see and hear. If it is true, if the boy she bore and lost has been found on a running track in London, every thought she has had about her fated life has been wrong.

"And into the water one last time. Oh no! A stumble! A stumble! But up again, back into to his rhythm, back into his stride. Come on Kembe! Come on! The crowd roar his name. The stadium is on its feet. It sounds like everyone in the country is cheering him along! Into the final hundred now, on the shoulder of the Ethiopian and gaining, eyes fixed on the tape. Come on Kembe! Come on Kembe! One man to beat, level, edging ahead and in front, a stride in front. The noise is deafening."

Mercy does not see her son cross the line first. She has collapsed onto the floor. A German couple are asking her if she is all right. The cheering and whooping British guests leap and jump into the air above her. They move from the screen enough for Mercy to see her son spring over the advertising boards and clamber across the seatbacks to his sister, her daughter.

"Lana," she says to the German lady who offers her a glass of water. "My beautiful girl." She sits up with her legs stretched out in front of her body. She looks like a fallen toddler, a child learning about the wonders of the world.

"Gold! Gold! Gold for Njenga!"

Now Mercy will stand up. She will stand up and walk to her room and shed her hotel uniform and throw the first clothes to hand and what few possessions she has into her suitcase. Then she will walk out along the staff corridor past the guest rooms past the lobby and out of the main entrance where employees are forbidden to exit. But this no longer matters as she has quit and will never return to this half-life. She will take a train to Frankfurt then board a plane to Heathrow. She will touch down on the same strip of tarmac that the son and daughter she had given up for dead came to earth upon seven long years ago in the search for their mother. A search that will end when the family of three stand together again, as though they had all risen up from the ground beneath their feet.

Wes Lee

The Dead Don't Do That Kind of Thing

"Deborah and I made a pact," Alison told Claire over the phone.

"What kind of pact?"

"When we were girls, whoever died first would come back and leave a sign."

Finger pressed on girlish finger - leaking blood. No! Claire didn't want to think about any pact that had been made without her.

"She was my twin!" Claire shouted.

The word felt terrible in her mouth, something fell away as she said it; halved and fell like a fleshy fruit – an overripe babaco. She tasted the sweet, slightly putrid hit at its core. My twin, she hadn't wanted to say it, she hadn't wanted to let it out, she hadn't wanted it to escape from her body and lose it forever. But Alison had made her say it. As if someone living, breathing in the world could be blind to the simple fact that Deborah had been her twin.

"Of course…but we were very close," Alison said.

"What do you want from me?" Her heart thumped in her chest. She tried to stop herself from shrieking.

"I thought it would give you comfort to know that she came back and left something for me."

Alison had told her she'd found snail-shells arranged in a circle on her doorstep the night after Deborah had died.

"Snails!"

"She loved snails."

She was making it up. Deborah wouldn't come back from the dead and leave snail-shells arranged in a fairy ring. It was some kind of wish fulfilment; Alison fixating on something that Deborah had said when they were children.

"Have you found anything unusual Claire?" Alison said.

"No!" She shouted as she slammed the phone down.

She wouldn't share it. Not with Alison.

*

Claire had noticed the bruises when she lay in the bath. Four dark fingerprints spread over her thigh. She'd felt a jolt when she'd seen them, like finding a lump in your breast or a black-hearted melanoma on your back; the horror of that second when you know you can never pretend again. The wineglass spins and smashes, the fender dents while reversing. She'd felt the hard smack at the centre of things. Her life had been full of moments like that.

She couldn't remember anything that could have imprinted her in that way. No strangely shaped furniture that she might have bumped against. They were definitely fingerprints.

She knew Deborah had made them. It wasn't the logical conclusion to draw, but she had been waiting for some kind of message over the weeks since Deborah had died. She'd been reading signs in everything, trying to birth them into being, but nothing had gelled the way that this did. She knew it – totally – she'd felt it in her body like a sharp stab, it wasn't her mind trying to conjure things.

Gary Silver, the medium she'd consulted, had told her that the bruises couldn't possibly be signs from the dead.

"The dead don't do that kind of thing," he said when she'd shown him the bruises.

"Why not?"

"They don't come back to hurt the living," he sneered.

Deborah had been reading one of his books in the hospice and she hadn't stopped talking about him. In the black and white headshot on the back of the book-jacket his eyes had looked neutral, impossible to read, staring out from a face that was as photogenic as a male model's. In person, he had the angriest eyes Claire had ever seen.

She'd thought that at least he'd listen to her; offer some kind of explanation – she supposed she'd wanted verification that the bruises were a sign that Deborah had visited her. She'd just wanted someone else to see them. But as soon as she'd mentioned the bruises, he'd bristled as if she'd been accusing him of something. She could see he was hostile to anything that contradicted his beliefs. What could she expect from a man who's latest book was called: We Do Not Die. No wonder it had become a bestseller.

"What about zombies? They fucking want to hurt the living," she said.

She could feel him scanning her, thinking the worst; that she was wallowing in some kind of morbid guilt. Survivor guilt.

"Why would your twin do something like that…did she hate you?"

"Not as much as you obviously do!" She shouted. She'd screamed expletives at him; roared at him in an unspeakable tongue, which he was probably used to hearing having a direct pipeline to the dead. She could imagine what kind of language they spoke – it wouldn't be polite, as most people didn't choose to join their ranks. Finding themselves amongst the dead after a car-crash, a heart attack, an operation botched – after the chest pounding, the injection of adrenalin, they'd found themselves somewhere they hadn't planned on being and no one was ever happy about that.

Fuck! Fuck! Fuck! The dead would shout. What the fuck happened to me!

The dead don't do that kind of thing.

"What a crock of shit!" She shouted at Gary Silver. "What a lousy faker you turned out to be!"

"Go hire yourself an exorcist!" He shouted as she'd travelled over his carpet and slammed the door to his office.

Why had she expected him to take her seriously? She was used to being misunderstood; used to being thought of as irrational. After all, she was the wild one, the bad twin, the one most likely to flip and end up in a mental institution; to run a pedestrian over while driving drunk in her car; to poison her father or hit her mother repeatedly with a plank; to have a teenage pregnancy and marry a man called Morgue. That's exactly what it's short for – a mortuary, a slab, the final drawer – the final fridge, an actual man called Morgue had told her when he'd introduced himself. But she hadn't done any of those things; although the mental institution thing she had flirted with, but she hadn't cared for any of their drugs. When she had taken them, gratefully at first – spinning crazy, so anxious and fucked-up and terribly afraid – they'd made her worse. They had spun her up to the next level, and the doctors had never managed to get it right. So guys with names like Morgue and Spider and Super had been her doctors - had given her the drugs. All the men she didn't marry. She'd found them and they had set her free; men with evil names had set her free; men with names her mother had hated had levelled her out – stoned her again and again, and she'd chased it – not the men, but the drugs. The men had been nothing compared to that sweet, blessed relief. And now she was clean, but it was hard being clean with all this death – first her mother, then Deborah. She didn't know how long she could stay away - feared every day she'd find herself whispering one of their names: Morgue, Spider, Snake, Super, Superman, Spiderman, Oh Spiderman.

And the dead one, Deborah, had been the good twin. No one ever shouted abuse at her. The shining sweet one, the white pure blank. How could two people bleed out of each other in such different ways – separate from one egg? When they were children, Deborah had wanted to be a nun while she had wanted to be a vampire. She'd told everyone that she wanted to sleep in a coffin and suck the blood of the living. When she grew up she had wanted to be undead.

Suck. Suck. Suck.

Deborah had seen a vision of a white lady as a child – standing in the middle of a glade filled with bluebells, pale and ghostly her mouth opening. Claire had watched Deborah reach out her hand; her eyes centered in the middle distance, a bright fervor on her face, but Claire had seen nothing, just a tree and the field and the sky – the look on her twin's face had scared her. After that, Deborah's face had taken on that blind Joan of Arc stare, like she was speaking to god or god was speaking to her.

Deborah and Alison had plotted to join a nunnery together, while Claire had dreamed of garlic wreaths, blood jellied eyes and gold crucifixes that would sear the flesh at her throat. Yet none of them had had the courage of their convictions; Deborah had ended up as a kindergarten teacher and Alison a Bank Manager.

Alison had hated Claire, she'd wanted Deborah all to herself. Poor chubby Alison - vampire meat; prey of vampires; food for the undead. When they were teenagers Claire had wanted to eat her, or at least take a big bite, having read that the biggest insult to anyone was to make them into food. Cannibals had relished that – eaten their enemies and defecated them out, knowing full well that it was the greatest affront to pass your enemy through your alimentary canal. It had been a cannibal curse in the Pacific – I ate your uncle! - a warrior would shout, targeting a man whose relative he'd eaten as he ran into battle. What purity. What a magnificent curse – our 21st century slurs paled before it. Motherfucker! Why fuck her when you could eat her and shit her out?

She could feel her mother turning over in her grave at that thought – feel her rolling. She'd be rolling her eyes, expecting nothing less from Claire, but smiling.

Yes – she'd be smiling. But not in that way that people always imagined the dead smile – not the sweet, simpering, sympathy-card-Hallmark-smile that people projected on the dead. The fake smile that people like Gary Silver made the dead wear.

The dead don't do that kind of thing.

Everything she'd read in Gary Silver's book about the dead coming back had said that the dead were enlightened. The dead were kind. The dead came back and smiled at the people they'd left behind; they beamed at them benevolently from the comfy chairs they'd inhabited when they were still alive. When people encountered the dead it was always nice. And they didn't always see them; the perfume that the dead had worn might suddenly fill the room. They might feel a hand brush their face and know that the dead had visited them. No one in his book had said they'd been whacked over the head by the dead, no one said they'd been suddenly slapped across the face with a newspaper. No one had felt bruises pushed into their thighs.

The dead don't do that kind of thing.

Why were the dead always smiling? Why were there were no angry faces on the other side? Why couldn't the dead leave bruises?

If her mother came back she would have an angry face. She had wanted to die in her own way - a non-believer in the hospice, not forced into some kind of deathbed conversion. She'd rejected all those passive, mystical smiles that the nurses courted on some of the other patients' faces. She'd said it was the nurses making it easy for themselves. Her mother had called those patients Mary's. She'd watched them straining to perfect the face of the Holy virgin – going out with a martyred smile.

Her mother wouldn't have a bar of it.

"I want to die pissed off with the world," her mother said. And Claire had known exactly what she'd meant, she'd seen her more clearly than she'd ever seen her in those last few weeks. Really seeing someone, that's what it was all about – not pushing your Pollyanna fantasies onto them. Respecting the hard things, not being scared to see them, and letting someone, her mother, express her anger.

But Deborah hadn't been able to do that. She didn't want to see it. She'd blanched when their mother got angry, she'd left the room. Deborah had pushed their mother into silence when she was in the room. Until her mother had tried on the Mary face for Deborah – a last hand stretched out towards her, a last grasp to keep her there.

Her mother had put on the Mary face for Deborah but with Claire she'd been able to be herself.

"I liked making the gardens, I hated the continual upkeep, what I really wanted was to make them and move on," she'd said. "I really just wanted to leave everything…I don't know why I stayed so long."

"For us," Claire said, but she knew, although she didn't say it, that she'd stayed for Deborah. You stayed for Deborah.

"You can't make dying pleasant, there's nothing good about it," her mother said, lifting the dressing on the wound on her stomach so that Claire could see it.

"The nurses pretend it's going to heal, they anoint it, they dress it, and some of them, the human ones, won't look in my eyes when they're doing it," her mother said. "I'll die before it heals, before it seals up again, before the cells get to do the job they've been doing selflessly all these years…mending me, putting me back together…"

She'd stared at Claire after she'd said it, and Claire's eyes had welled up; tears had dropped on her mother's blankets; big silent hopeless tears. Claire had wanted it to heal, she'd wanted her to be put back together, she'd swallowed down all the sadness and sourness and bitterness and had let her be angry. She'd let her be all the things she had wanted to be in the end. She'd been her witness and it was such a raw fucked-up feeling she was left with.

Maybe she had wanted to see the Mary face, maybe she had wanted her mother to put it on for her. Maybe it was easier that way for the people left behind, if they see, if they remember, the Mary face.

"Don't open the curtains," her mother said. "It's better in the dark. I don't want to see out there."

And Deborah would stride into the room, pull back the curtains and announce brightly, "How are you?" Forcing their mother to make some kind of false report – the sun in her eyes, squinting at Deborah.

"A little better today."

"Why can't you let her be angry?" Claire asked Deborah.

"Because if she'd open up a crack and let the light in she'd see things differently. But you're the one keeping her here, in her arrested development. You aren't letting her grow."

"She's not fucking growing, she's dying," Claire said.

"I've seen people change in here…I've seen people so filled with joy that their hearts have almost leapt out of their bodies. I know the kinds of things that can happen to people."

"Not people, our mother."

"Deborah has a strong faith," her mother told Claire. "She's luckier than us."

She'd tried to tell Deborah things that their mother had said. She'd tried to share the connection that had been so strong towards the end. But her mother had put on the Mary face for Deborah, she'd gone out smiling for Deborah.

*

"How are you?" Alison said over the phone.

"Counting down the seconds to the cocktail hour," Claire said.

"I'm sure no one's watching."

"Please stop calling."

Alison had told her that she'd built a little shrine around the snail-shells. Claire imagined Alison lining them up like a grotesque nativity scene. She'd said that one of the snails – a tiny pale one – had begun to weep blood.

"We're having a celebration for Deborah, everyone is coming over to see my shrine. Gary's putting it in his new book, he's doing a whole chapter on Deborah. He's televising it in a one hour special."

Claire knew that Gary Silver would never mention the bruises. They would make an unholy alliance - Alison and Monsieur Silver – it was fitting in a way, Claire thought.

She imagined Alison onstage with him, preening like a game-show participant. Wallowing in her fifteen minutes of fame:

"And Deborah was your childhood friend, your best friend?" Gary would announce into the microphone.

"That's right Gary," Alison would say.

"You said you found the snails arranged on your doorstep, the night after she passed."

"That's correct Gary."

"A message is coming through . . . I'm hearing something, it's a message from Deborah."

Claire heard the scream. Her own scream in her ears, filling up the high-vaulted chamber of the television studio. She saw herself planted in the audience, roaring down to the stage like a rabid chimpanzee, screaming that Alison had made it all up – tipping over the carefully arranged nativity scene like a chessboard. Clutching Alison's throat, her fingers deep in her flesh, leaving dark, incontrovertible bruises on her neck.

She couldn't believe that man was writing a chapter on Deborah – immortalizing her, making Deborah into a saint. And the nurses at the hospice, they'd wanted to beatify her too – deify her saintly fucking death.

When their mother had died, Claire hadn't been able to find a nurse anywhere, it was as if they'd had a sixth sense about her death, the corridors had been empty. Her mother was right, they only wanted to be there for the good deaths, and really, who could blame them. Her mother had been terrified, but she wouldn't let go and Claire had whispered for her to let go; to just let go, and her mother's eyes had been so frightened. Deborah had been nowhere to be found, she hadn't been able to reach her anywhere.

When they were children, Claire had lifted Deborah out of bed in the middle of the night and had laid her across the doorway of their bedroom – she'd tried to sacrifice her. But it wasn't Deborah that the monster had wanted, he'd passed over her. He'd wanted the one he couldn't break, the one who'd been defiant, the one who wouldn't smile when their mother had brought him into their house; eager to fill the slot of the brand new father. Deborah would wake in the morning on the carpet, cold and groggy not knowing how she'd got there, and Claire would tell her she'd been sleepwalking. Claire had been the one he'd wanted and she had never told her mother what he'd done – she'd always known she'd spare her that.

"I never want to see your fucking snails," she told Alison

"I'm just reaching out a hand to let you know I'm here."

"If you call again I'll get a restraining order."

"People have the right to see them…she wasn't just yours."

"I don't fucking want you to put them on television."

"People want to believe…let them believe," Alison said.

For the first time Claire heard the strain in her voice; the thing swimming underneath – the doubt. The doubt! She heard it clearly in her voice. Alison was afraid.

"We do not die," Alison said quickly, like a mantra, as if words could brazen it out in the face of death; like a shield, a sentence used to fight it.

We do not die. That's what Deborah had said in the hospice, right to the end she'd believed it – dying with that beatific smile on her face. All the nurses around her plumping her pillows as if she was Ashley Wilkes's martyred wife in Gone with the Wind.

Why am I resisting, Claire thought? Why don't I just let it happen? Let them all believe the Mary face, let them have what they want, what they need.

*

Claire opened the door of her mother's art deco cabinet, she'd been bringing shells back from the beach since Deborah had died and laying them out on the shelves – the smell of the sea contained like that hit her strongly – it smelt like the Natural History section at the museum – sharp ammonia and dry decay. Whenever they had visited the museum as children they'd held their noses, giggling and elbowing each other as they followed their mother around. She leant in through the doors and breathed it in.

We set up all our surprises she thought.

She took out her mother's silver brooch, fashioned in the shape of a flower. A bee centered in the middle of it – soldered at the end of a wire so that when the wearer touched the brooch, the bee moved as if it was hovering over it. When they were children they would breathe on it and see if they could make it move; the wire was so fine that if you blew hard enough the bee trembled. And Deborah had said she'd seen god's hand in that bee; something quivering with hope as if it could take off, as if it was at the beginning of something – ready to fly and waiting for the right moment when it would lift. Had she seen it too? She couldn't remember feeling the wonder but she'd seen it on her twin's face, she'd seen it in her eyes.

"A trembling bee…that's all we are," she whispered and blew gently on it – it still trembled. It looked like a quaking frightened thing, something captured; it was tarnished and needed a clean. Her mother had always kept it polished, she'd put her jewelry away in the dark to make it stay shiny longer. She'd wrapped her handbags in plastic; the ones she'd kept for best, and her shoes in boxes, everything kept to last forever.

Claire picked out the embroidered jewelry box that Deborah had been working on in the hospice. She hadn't really paid much attention to what Deborah was embroidering on it – flowers, a garden scene – a figure surrounded with light; that day she'd seen the white lady amongst the bluebells. She ran her fingers over the lid; traced the outlines of the bright blue flowers. Funny what becomes important at the end of our lives. She wondered what would become important to her – re-reading a favorite book – seeing a much loved film? Would she fight to get to the video store against all odds, drag herself onto the bus and sit there knowing she was dying; seeing all the life going on around her and no one else knowing how important those mo-ments were? It probably happened every day, if you looked around you'd see those faces; compelled to go to a favorite garden, a much loved spot, maybe feed the ducks for what they thought might be the last time – some parting gesture, some parting shot. What would she do? What would she get close to when it was her time, assuming that she knew? She'd been around too many people who'd known they were dying lately, she realised she'd just assumed she'd know; that she'd be waiting like her mother and Deborah in their different ways.

Vanessa Gebbie

Dodie's Gift

There is a little blood on the sand, in a hollow in the dunes. There is semen too, although it is hidden in the shadows where sand and grass have been churned. The blood is clear, scarlet, bright; both its colour and its brightness out of place in the soft grey-green and pale straw colours here. It will fade soon, darken until it's almost black, and it will be lost when a herring gull chooses this place to bring the head of a newly dead catfish. He will drop it, stand over it, stabbing at it with his yellow hooked beak, parting skin from muscle, lip from cheek, eye from socket, until all that is left is a mess of reddened bone and one thin sliver of catfish skin with a feeler still attached.

There are tracks leading in different directions. One set, Dodie's, scramble up the side of the dune, the sand puddled and broken where she tried to claw her way out of the hollow, the top slipping further away with every step. The marram grasses are crushed where she slid down towards the field. The barley stubble is also crushed, over, over, over, where Dodie ran crying to the General Stores.

The other footmarks are The Philosopher's, weighted, regular, the sand only disturbed and uneven in one spot at the base of the slope where he stood to adjust his clothing before striding away towards the caravan site.

**

Who is Dodie? Just this: a woman in her forties who works at the Stores. Invisible. She wears a blue nylon overall, and if it is hot she is uncomfortable by the end of the day. Maybe she smells of onions. She sleeps above the Stores in a small room that overlooks the yard. She's worked here as long as the surfers and body boarders who stay at the caravan site can remember. If you find her at the Tinner's Arms in the evening, you'll see she doesn't drink much, makes half a cider last all evening, but Bill at the Tinner's doesn't mind. She's a fixture who has a place here, whereas in a city she would drown.

It is difficult to give a name to what makes Dodie different. There is no lack of intelligence, with her appetite for reading of all sorts, crosswords, number puzzles. But it is as though a membrane separates Dodie from the world. As though she was born covered in a caul which was never quite stripped away. She looks at you, puzzled, trying to work you out, trying to read you, know you.

What she does know is here, in the Stores. She knows

the pastel and black plastic tops of deodorants and the gold, white and green of hairsprays. She knows the sugary smell of Lux soap, the deeper elusive scent of Imperial Leather. She knows the jolly primary colours of perfect cereal bowls on the packets of own brand and Kelloggs. She knows how sticky soap powder feels if it spills out of the box.

Dodie reads everything. Everything that comes in to the Stores in twine-tied bundles brought by the paper van. Newspapers. Women's magazines, white smiles on the cover, *'How to cook for six on a shoestring'*, *'Sex after the menopause? It's great!'* Men's magazines with bottoms and breasts pushing out on the front cover. Children's comics. Puzzle books. She uses the photocopier in the back to copy the puzzles. Fishing periodicals. Surfing magazines. Music magazines. The special stamp-collecting issue that comes in for Mr. Fisher next to the Church Hall. She takes them up to her room and reads them all, careful not to mark them, then pushes them under the mattress to flatten them and puts them on the shelves the next day.

Who is The Philosopher? Just this: a man in late middle age, like a million others, greying, spreading, unremarkable. Invisible too. He came into the General Stores towards the end of a day in mid-September, and stood by the bread racks. He put one hand up to a Mother's Pride plastic wrapper, and just stood there, head bowed, his rucksack making it difficult for other shoppers to pass easily. Dodie waited for a while before coming out from behind the counter.

"What are you doing?" she said, glancing at his face,

then away.

The man looked up at the bread, then at her.

"I'm thinking," he said. "I'm thinking about bread."

"OK, but could you think over there?"

The man did not smile, although his eyes narrowed a little and it could have been a smile coming. Dodie had read that smiles start with the eyes. But if she had looked closer, there were no laughter lines. He took a loaf of bread and moved to the till. Dodie took his money without a word. From then on he was, to her at any rate, The Philosopher.

**

They know little about each other after a few days of him appearing in the Stores, standing there, thinking. He chooses his times. Chooses times when the Stores isn't too busy, so he can stand and think. Because he knows it intrigues her.

She has no idea who he is. Just a man, slightly over-weight, staying on the caravan site (she asked), cheap deal, last minute. Caravan sleeping four, but he's only one. He goes for long walks, alone. She's seen him in The Tinner's, drinking beer out of a bottle like a teen-ager. She asked his name "Mr...can't remember," someone said.

She imagines him shaving in the morning in pyjama bottoms, peering into a speckled mirror that spots his face. He has a mouth that might have turned up once, now it is pinched. His hair is faded, was reddish. Thinning. His eyebrows are a straggle of too-long hairs. He looks wild, energetic. But that may be just illusion.

Now Dodie's thinking too. She's thinking she's never met anyone like this. He stands there in the Stores at different times, day after day, where she can see him, but she's sure he hasn't stood there deliberately. By the bread one day, the tinned food, the next. He sat on the floor once with his head in hands. He is so deep, she thinks. So lost in thought. He was thinking about bread that first time. *Bread.* What about bread? A fundamental of life? Biblical? What, Mother's Pride? Then *tinned food?* Thinking about tinned food? Time, that must be it, with tinned food. Preserving time. Keeping things unspoiled, but in the dark where you can't see them, and they can't see you. Baked beans, own brand cheaper than Heinz. Tomatoes, dented tins cut price. It must all mean something.

Dodie thinks this must have been coming for a long time. She hasn't exactly been waiting for it, more it has been waiting to happen. She knows she's clever, because they told her, years ago at school, she won prizes. Books, with stickers in. Bookmarks. A painted plate.

The Philosopher has been coming for a long, long time. It's been in her horoscope. Over and over she's read it: *"Virgo: With the moon in Mercury, you're going through a difficult time in your love life. But your time will come. Your even temperament will please someone who needs you."*

Dodie the *Virgo.* She knows, because she's read it so

many times… *"Only 5% of females are still virgins at the age of forty-five."*

She's forty-five before Christmas.

**

Today The Philosopher stands by the washing powders, fabric conditioner and Fairy Liquid. It's nearly closing time, and Dodie needs to mark some unsold goods with today's sell-by date at half price. She needs to walk past him to collect two Mother's Prides and some malt loaf, some wedges of "Farmer's Own Choice" cheese and a four pack of cherry yogurt. He says nothing as she passes him. But when she comes back, he's blocking the aisle.

"Excuse me," she says.

He says nothing but moves back. Then, when Dodie is touching him with her arms, holding the goods close to her breasts, because he has not moved quite far enough, he says, his voice so close to her ear that she jumps,

"I'm still thinking."

"What about?"

"Guess."

Dodie looks round, sees a Fairy Liquid bottle. "Recycling?" she says, "Reincarnation?"

The Philosopher smiles, kind of. "How clever," he says.

"We are on the same wavelength."

"Are we?" says Dodie, nonplussed, putting half-price stickers on the malt loaf. The Philosopher puts a hand on the loaf, catching two of her fingers under his. She jumps again. His breath smells sweet-heavy.

"I'll have this," he says. "And that," he nods his head at the bread and cheese, "when you've finished." He waits.

Dodie adds the prices up wrong. Blushes.

"When you've finished…" he repeats.

"Sorry…"

"…we could talk about thinking. At the pub."

"Sorry?"

"Well?"

She was right. It was coming. He was always coming, and she should have been ready. He'd seen something in her that she hasn't met herself yet, and she didn't *see* it. "…*your time will come. Your even temperament…*"

"Yes please." Dodie says. And knowing she smells of onions, "Half an hour?"

And Dodie starts to make herself ready. Not just herself, although this is unconscious. Her room is as tired as she is. The bed slumps; what was bright pink candlewick is faded, uneven, the fringe pulled, trailing on the rug. There is a framed print above the bed of the sea crashing against rocks; someone, a long time back, pencilled a boat in one corner. She tried to rub it out but it's still there, a stick man waving through the ocean at her. Dodie takes down the unlined cotton curtains and takes off the bedspread, bundles them together and puts them in the downstairs washing machine. That makes her feel better.

Later, in The Tinners, they sit together in Dodie's corner, on sagging burgundy plush cushions. He has bought her a cider, he drinks beer from the bottle. They talk. Dodie is half listening, looking at the scratches through the varnish on the table…the number four among the scratches.

Bill calls over. "Dodie? You OK, love?"

The Philosopher answers, before she does, "She's fine." Dodie just looks up and smiles.

"Look," Dodie says, tracing the scratches with her finger. "Number four."

"It will mean something," he says. "You wait…"

And Dodie waits, breathlessly, drinking in instances of the number four the next day. Four silver cars in a row outside the General Stores. Four stamps on a letter from New Zealand awaiting collection under the counter of the post office shelf. Four brown moles on her left thigh. Four packets of condoms sold to the driver of the paper van.

..

She's picking up some apples that have fallen onto the floor. A voice close to her ear, a hand on her shoulder…"So what did the number mean?" Dodie drops the apples. Four of them.

"I don't know…" she breathes.

"Yes you do," he says. "You have the gift."

Dodie straightens up, the apples in her hands. "Have I?" she says, eyes bright.

And so it goes on. Dodie's curtains are re-hung. She cleans her room over and over, getting down on her knees to wipe the skirting board with a blue cloth. She buys herself some hair colour, first time ever. Chestnut lights, it says, and it splashes in the sink, works its way into the cracks round the plughole. Leaves her hairline looking dark, dark. She tries the lipsticks, buys a chalky pink one, *Moonflower.*

Bill at the pub keeps asking if she's OK. She smiles every time.

Four days. They've been 'going out' for four days, and people are smiling at Dodie, not at The Philosopher, and she thinks they mind about something. Maybe they are jealous because not everyone can think so deeply. Today, today, today and today. Four of them. He's so clever. He thinks about hedges, drainage ditches, yellow diggers, dead crows, sheep's wool, and seaweed. He says there is so much to think about in this life.

Dodie breathes faster. She searches for things, finds

them, throws things out for him to think about.

"What about beermats? Darts? Chipped pint mugs? Alcopops? Boiled eggs? Coffee?"

The Philosopher smiles and pats her hand. She doesn't jump any more. "Some things are deeper than others," he says. "I'll teach you."

And she listens looking through him, her lower *Moonflower* lip hanging loose as he thinks in streams about newspapers, printing ink and trees, the 'circle' as he calls it of capitalism (where, he says, lots of people work in a circle, or a spiral, doing things made necessary by the 'work' done by the person before, but take them all out, and the world wouldn't suffer). Sometimes he bangs the table with his fist and her cider jumps and Bill looks over and raises an eyebrow.

**

It's late on the fourth day. She's going for a walk with The Philosopher today. He's coming for her soon, half an hour after closing time he said, seven thirty they close. Eight he'll come. They'll walk down the lane towards the beach, and they will think as they go about bungalows, lamp posts, telegraph poles maybe. *Communication*. That's it. Tarmac, double yellow lines and crows flying high up above the bent fir trees. Wind. She'll ask him what wind is, because you can feel it, but can't see it, and that must be like God. Or is it the world turning faster and faster and faster so in the end everyone will fall over? She laughs at the thought and feels the power of it.

Dodie remakes her bed and buys herself some freesias from the bucket outside the door of the Stores. Yellow like slab cheddar. And lilac. She cuts the stems, puts them in a handleless mug painted with a boat flying the Cornish flag, and the freesias splay out on the chest of drawers, hanging in her room like aliens. She showers, using a new shower gel the girl surfers buy, which smells of lemons and limes. She puts on a flowered skirt she hasn't worn for years, a white blouse. *Moon-flower.*

The lane is quiet. They pass the bungalows, and just as she knew they would they think about bungalows. About old people, zimmer frames and holiday-makers, buckets of dead whelks. They pass the telegraph poles, wires, and she was right, they think about the buzz of conversation, and she brings in God then, about how God can differentiate between prayers and ordinary conversation. About whether whispering is a better way to communicate than shouting, about letters from New Zealand that no-one picks up, and she's sure it's a woman's writing.

They pass the barley field and think about the razored stalks, about harvest mice displaced, and she feels the sadness of it.

They walk on to the beach, the sea pounding to their left, the dunes on their right. They pass three herring gulls tearing at a dead catfish, and they think about pre-dation, food chains, starving and feasting. The beach is empty, and it's getting cold. The sun is still up there, just.

..

The Philosopher has been holding her hand. His grip tightens a little and she starts to think about her room, the curtains, how the sun will come through the curtains early in the morning, the freesias. The stick man in his boat. She wants to tell The Philosopher about the stick man, because it must mean something, and he says, "Let's sit down here," pulling her towards the dunes. But Dodie doesn't want to go there. She wants to go back to her room, because her horoscope did say, "...*your time will come. Your even temperament will please someone who needs you.*"

But he doesn't listen. He's not saying what he's thinking any more, and their footsteps, which had left regular tracks in the damp, flat sand right to where the waves are beating, become crossed, muddled, fast.

Dodie stumbles on the dry sand of the dunes as he pulls her up the side. 'Why?" she says. "Why are we going here?" and she says something about freesias and stick men and The Philosopher says nothing, just pulls, pushes, doesn't even look at her face, pulls, pushes, pulls, pushes and hurts her.

**

He doesn't come in to the General Stores the next day.

At the end of that day, Dodie walks down the lane, waiting for the thoughts to come. She passes the bungalows, and they are just bungalows, their windows blank. The telegraph poles carry wires that hum in the wind. The barley stalks have cut her legs. She walks along the beach, looking to see if the tide has left any footsteps. They are there, somewhere, she thinks, even though their shape has gone.

She sees a young couple walking, the girl's hair blowing over her face like a veil, and she feels the sadness of that.

She waits for them to pass and climbs slowly up the dune, searching. The grasses are still flat, but the breeze has softened the shadows in the sand. The place is healing itself. But there, at the bottom of the hollow, a gull has had a meal, and the sand holds white bone, red bone, skin, and Dodie doesn't want to see it.

She tries to make something out of yesterday's incident that is not hopeless. She won't allow herself to name the act that happened here, and will wonder, if someone takes something you were going to give them anyway, is that stealing? She will think. In time her thoughts will become memories, and she will recall a little kindness where in fact there was little, and some meaning where there was none at all.

Jonathan Attrill

Felipe and the Sea

Felipe lived in a nameless town in the centre of a country that did not exist. He lived with his grandmother in a small house that sighed when the wind blew. His father had been killed whilst Felipe was still a baby, fighting in a magnificent war of noble causes (although no one could remember what those causes were any longer) and his mother had died two years previously from a strain of influenza that attacked only mothers of single children.

Apart from the death of his mother, Felipe was happy with his life in the town. He went to the only school there was and enjoyed learning about strange animals he'd never seen and even stranger people. After school finished he would wander off to play in the jungle with his best friend Angelica. They would mimic the sounds of parrots and monkeys and climb the huge trees together. He even loved the heavy rains that would fall for two or three days until the streets were mud. He had only one regret.

Felipe had never seen the sea.

He knew the sea existed because he'd read about it in books. He knew the sea was blue, or sometimes green or even grey; he knew it tasted of salt; he knew it brought a breeze and that squealing birds called seagulls hovered about its waters. More than this, travellers would sometimes come through the town as they journeyed across the mountains on their way to somewhere or other that did have a name, and they would bring tales of the sea with them. Once a group of gringos came through and told the town's people how they had been shipwrecked. The sea had risen like a great monster one night, tearing their ship to shreds as if it were no more than a toy, killing most of the crew and passengers. They were the lucky few who had survived, washed up on the shore, and now they were travelling across the mountains searching for somewhere they could start a new life from scratch. Felipe found this story terrifying, but it only increased his fascination with the sea.

Gypsies often passed through, too, on their way to nowhere in particular. They were the best storytellers of all, with their tales of midnight fires crackling on the beaches as they sang and danced while the surf came and went in soft whooshes, leaving crabs on the sand which they would roast for breakfast as the dawn turned the sea from black to gold. They believed they were a race of people born in the sea which was why, if you looked very closely, you could still see the healed-over remains of gills which had been in full working order on their ancient ancestors.

Yet others brought tales of pirates and adventure on the high seas; treasure buried at the bottom of the ocean; multi-coloured forests beneath the waves; mermaids with white hair and shimmering scales; creatures that spouted water from their heads and were as big as a row of houses; gigantic fish with teeth the size of a man's fist; sea serpents and other monsters of the deep with many arms and bulging eyes.

More than anything, it was the incredible variety of the sea that attracted Felipe. He knew it could soothe or destroy, give life or bring death, whisper quietly or rage like a madman, and that its winds could transform themselves from gentle breezes into ferocious hurricanes. Felipe loved the jungle but he longed for the sea. His grandmother was old and he was all she had left in this world so he could not leave the town and travel to the sea, the lover he longed for. Felipe was a boy, but a boy on the verge of manhood and he was beginning to learn of such things.

Often Felipe would visit the little church of Father Santiago to confess his sinful thoughts. The priest was a very old man, so wrinkled he looked like a nut, his skin brown and leathery. He was as old as the town and some said he'd founded it. He had certainly brought the knowledge of Jesus's sufferings for the redemption of humanity to the people. The priest had great kindness and was never severe, never recommending more than a few 'Hail Mary's' and 'Our Father's' to Felipe, even when he believed that he deserved to be given a much greater penance.

On this particular day, however, as Felipe sat on the stool in the sweltering heat of the little cubicle, shielded from the solemn eyes of Father Santiago, he felt rather more strange than guilty.

'What is it that's bothering you, my son?' the priest asked. 'Remember, there is nothing that the Lord does not have the mercy to forgive. Have you been having impure thoughts again?'

'Not exactly, Father?' Felipe replied. He did not know how to put it into words. 'It is about my friend, Angelica.'

'Ah,' the priest said, as if he understood already.

'When we used to play together it was like we were just the same. We swam together in the river, we teased the monkeys, we played hide and seek in the jungle. But now…'

'Go on.'

'Now I look at her and I see the way that her hair flows, the sparkle in her eyes, the smile that seems so sad but fills me with happiness. When I am near her I can feel my heart like a little bird inside my chest. I do not understand, Father. Am I a sinner for looking on her in such a way, or is she a witch?'

'No, Felipe, she is not a witch, though I believe she has unknowingly bewitched you. And you are certainly not a sinner. There is no sin in love.'

Love! Was that what it was when he looked at Angelica? Was that what it was when he could not sleep for thinking about her? It seemed impossible that he could love the person who had been his best friend for as long as he could remember. 'So, I am in love,' he thought dejectedly, as if it was the worst catastrophe that could have struck him. He knew what love meant. Marriage and children. Felipe still harboured thoughts that one day, after his grandmother had passed away, he could leave the town and travel to the faraway ocean. Now he saw that dream slipping away.

Over the next few weeks Felipe tried hard to fight

against this plague of love that had infected him. He avoided Angelica as much as he possibly could, so that in the end she stopped coming to ask if he wanted to come out and play with her. But it was no cure. His infection only grew worse. Now Angelica was there in his dreams, too, and when he woke he felt feverish. Strange butterflies swarmed about him everywhere he went so that people even started to call him The Butterfly Boy instead of Felipe. His grandmother would catch as many as she could each day in a net and release them in the jungle, but the very next morning a hundred more had taken their place as if Felipe had brought them back from his dreams.

He could cope with the fevers and the butterflies but what Felipe could not cope with was the memory of that look in Angelica's eyes as he'd turned her away from his door all those times. She must think that he hated her and whenever that thought overtook him a pain would shoot through his body from the top of his head to his feet as if a lightning bolt had struck him. Indeed, when the pain had passed he often found the top of his head sizzling and scorch-marks beneath his feet.

Then came the rain.

As bad as the rains were in the town this rain was worse. It would not stop. Four days, one week, two weeks went by, and still it poured. If things went on much longer the whole town would be washed away. Felipe noticed that people were beginning to give him strange looks and whispering about him as he passed by. Sometimes he heard them saying things such as, 'There he goes, it's all his fault. Ever since those butterflies started hovering around him there's been nothing but bad luck in this town.' He knew they hated him.

One evening Felipe was resting on his bed when his grandmother came into his room. 'Felipe,' she said, 'Father Santiago is here to see you.'

Felipe did not speak. His face was turned to the wall, but he heard the door softly close and he knew Father Santiago was still there in the room with him. He could hear the old man's breathing and smell his odour of vanilla.

'Felipe,' the priest began, 'I must speak with you. These rains are beginning to weary the people. If they go on much longer there will be no town left. People are growing restless and they believe it's something to do with you; they want to take the law into their own hands.'

Felipe turned. The priest was drenched. The butterflies that always accompanied Felipe fluttered around the priest's head but he took no notice. Felipe saw the concern in his eyes.

'Let them kill me,' Felipe said. 'I do not care. Perhaps in heaven I will be able to visit the sea.'

'Ah yes, the sea.' Everyone knew of Felipe's great love. 'You are young, you still have a lifetime ahead in which you can experience the sea.'

'Not if I am married. Then I will never leave this town.'

Father Santiago nodded slowly. 'I think I am beginning to understand,' he said. 'You know sometimes, Felipe, love comes to us. Many years ago the Lord came to me. I did not ask him to come, but he came all the same.'

'The sea will not come to me.'

'No, that is true,' the old man said. 'Very true. But it is also true that when love does come to us, you must embrace it with all your being. You asked me about sin the last time you came to confession, Felipe, and I will tell you a secret. I believe there is only one true sin, and it is this: when love knocks on the door of your heart it is a sin to turn it away.'

The priest left Felipe alone in the darkened room, listening to the thrumming of the fat raindrops on the roof.

An hour later, after ruminating on the old man's words, Felipe climbed out of his bedroom window and crept through the town. He could barely see through the lashing rain and fell face first into the swilling mud on more than one occasion. Now and then a dog sheltering under a piece of tin in a backyard barked at him, as if telling him he must be mad, not even a dog would be out on such a night. But Felipe went on.

At last he came to Angelica's house.

He sloshed through the mud and up to her window.

Inside it was dark but he could make out her sleeping form on the bed. 'Angelica,' he whispered. She stirred in her sleep but did not wake.

His heart pounding along with the rain, Felipe hopped into the room. If Angelica's father caught him in her room in the darkness he might shoot him, thinking he was a robber. Carefully he crept to her bedside.

The light in the room was dim but he could still see her face, the soft dark hairs around the corners of her mouth, the shadows of her cheekbones, the curve of her eyebrows. A powerful scent filled his nostrils and he did not know if it came from the jungle flowers, made stronger by the rain, or Angelica herself. She was sleeping but her eyes flickered behind the lids and he prayed she was dreaming of him. He stroked her hair, dark as a midnight ocean, and felt the blood surging through his veins like a hidden current. 'Angelica,' he murmured. He bent and touched her mouth with his own. It was then he felt the waters of the faraway ocean washing over him, tasted its salt on his lips, swam in its depths, and knew he would never long for the sea again.

Laura Solomon

Alternative Medicine

Halfway through his second year at medical school, my brother David took a job as a dancing bear. He proudly announced his new vocation one Sunday, over one of our mother's vegan roast dinners; peppers, spuds, pumpkin, drizzled in olive oil and sprinkled with rosemary and rock salt.

"I've taken a little part-time work as a dancing bear," he said. "Just shopping malls and kids' parties. It's easy work and surprisingly well-paid. In fact, I'm kind of starting to wonder why I'm bothering with medical school at all. Maybe I could just quit and go full time as a bear. Pass me the hummus would you Mum?"

Our mother nearly choked on her slice of whole-meal bread.

"A bear?" she scoffed. "I didn't shell out on those exorbitant fees so that you could go galavanting round the town dressed up as a *bear*."

David stood his ground.

"It's not *galavanting*, it's good work. Hard graft. The

kids love it. They respond instinctively to my furry paws and kindly nature. My growl is not frightening, but soft. More of a purr, really. On the bear scale, I'm closer to Teddy than Grizzly."

Dad continued to calmly eat his dinner. His wife was not quite so composed.

"Oh David," she said. "Why do you have to be a bear? Why can't you just take some casual bar work? Or apply for a larger student loan?"

"I like the job. It makes a pleasant change from aortas and tibias and fibulae."

Silence.

"Well," said Mum, eventually, "it's your life dear. You do what you like with it. Larry, would you switch on the radio please?"

I did as I was told. Nothing more was said about the bear that evening.

Several weeks later, my mother found the heart in the freezer. She was feeling tired and, having come to the conclusion that this could well be due to a lack of iron, she had decided to make a spinach tortilla for her lunch. Three years previously, at her insistence, the whole family had turned pescatarian or vegaquarian; call it what you will, we ate only fish and vege's. She said that fish was good for the brain; every night she gave us spoonfuls of cod liver oil. I would hold mine in my mouth, then run to the upstairs bathroom and spit it out. David always swallowed his.

At our house, we had two freezers; a small unit above the fridge, and a larger deep freeze in the garage, which is where the heart was found, underneath a bag of scallops, nestled up against a lobster that had sat there, uneaten, for the last decade. The heart was in a blue plastic bag, coated with that fine white ice you get when you haven't defrosted in a while. She didn't realise what it was at first. She thought it was a piece of old steak or liver, bought long ago, in the meat-eating days, forgotten, now rediscovered. She took it upstairs and put it in the microwave on low, stood watching the plate revolving in the glow of that dull, artificial light. When she considered it sufficiently thawed, she took it from its bag and laid it on a plate. It was then that she recognised the organ. Not the stylised Valentine's Day tomato-red ticker, with the two curves at the top, like a woman's breasts, narrowing to a single point, but a solid lump of meat, dark red, almost brown. If you looked closely enough, you could see the valves. She had no recollection of buying such a thing herself, but assumed that somebody, Dad or David, must have, years ago, purchased an ox's heart, intending to make some kind of stew perhaps, or a satay. It wasn't until that evening that she discovered that this heart was not animal, but human.

We ate together as a family every night, sitting at the dining room table. My mother thought it helped us to communicate with one another. I was envious of other families, who ate in front of the television with plates positioned on trays or, more precariously, on their laps. We didn't have a TV to watch; my father said that it rotted the brain. It was usually my mother who kicked off the conversation. This night was no exception.

"You'll never guess what I found in the freezer this afternoon," she began.

"What, the deep freeze?" asked Dad. "Surprised you can find anything in there. Needs a good clean out, that does."

"A heart," she said. "Whom does it belong to?"

"Oh yeah," said David. "I was going to tell you about that. What did you do with it?"

"It's on the kitchen bench. Is it a cow's heart?"

"No, human."

"What on *earth* did you bring it home for? Assuming, of course, that you got it from the medical school and haven't been digging up the graves of the recently deceased in order to rob them of their vital organs."

"I was intending to pickle it."

"To *pickle* it?"

"Yeah, chuck it in some formaldehyde. I thought it could serve as a kind of study aid, you know."

"Oh David. Couldn't you just have left it at the university?"

David shrugged.

"I didn't think you'd mind," he said, pushing back his chair and rising to his feet. "Anyway, I'm going out for a bit."

Our mother looked alarmed.

"Where are you going, dear? I thought we could all play a nice game of Scrabble this evening."

"Got a bear appointment," came the mumbled reply.

"At this time of night?"

"Eighteenth birthday party. In a bar downtown."

"Isn't eighteen a little too old for dancing bears?"

"They're payin', I'm playin'."

"Well, please try to be quiet when you come in."

"Will do. See you later. Put the heart back in the freezer, will you?"

He bent down and gave her a little peck on the cheek.

..

Three weeks later she discovered the brain in a box beneath David's bed. Unlike the heart, it was not frozen. She found it when she was vacuuming his room – she only did under the beds once a month. She knew that she should leave the box alone, yet, against her better nature, she opened it anyway. There it sat, a lump of broiled grey cauliflower, a three pound universe. An internal map that had once reflected somebody's external world, but that now sat inert, mindless. She put the lid back on the box, put the box back under the bed.

At the dinner table that night, she said, "David, was that a brain I found under your bed today?"

"Oh," said my brother. "Thanks for reminding me. I need to get onto preserving that. I've brought all the kit home; the latex, the formalin. I just keep procrastinating."

My mother put down her knife and fork and folded her arms.

"David," she said firmly. "I know that you're a medical student, but I don't want my house filled with human organs. It's macabre."

"It's not *macabre*. It's part of life, part of death. It's the body. Everybody's got one; you've got one, I've got one."

"But what if we have visitors David? Nobody wants to walk into your room by accident and find a brain in a jar. Or a pickled heart."

"I'll keep them in the wardrobe. Jesus Mum! I know you've stumbled across these things, but it's only because you're always prodding about in various corners of the house. It's not like I leave them lying about the place. Gimme a break, would ya? Anyway."

Scrape. The sound of his chair legs across the floor.

"Bear gig calling. See ya tomorrow morning."

He picked up the bear suit that he kept hung on a hook by the door. A second later, we heard the engine of his car splutter into life and he roared off down the road. My mother turned to her husband.

"You know, Cliff," she said. "I really would appreciate it if you would back me up on these things, instead of just sitting there shovelling lentil pie into your mouth."

"Don't take it out on me, love."

"But don't you think it's odd that he brings these things home?"

"Harmless, love, harmless. Ignore it. Better that than shooting up heroin in some dark alley, right?"

He reached out and gave her hand a squeeze then retired to the living room to read his evening paper.

"It's this bloody bear thing," my mother muttered, more to herself than to me. "He never used to bring this garbage home before he had that ridiculous job."

She cleared the dining room table, than began furiously cleaning the kitchen benches, as if all her worries could be scrubbed away with a bit of Crème Cleanser and a scouring cloth.

There was a femur in the medicine cabinet; it was small, a child's. It was me that found it. I had been helping my mother make apple and rhubarb pie, clumsily chopping up Granny Smiths, when I had accidentally given myself a nasty cut on the thumb and run to the bathroom in search of a sticking plaster. There it was, propped up on the bottom shelf like some weird tribal offering. It sat next to a rusting blue razor. I took a plaster from the box, wrapped it round my cut thumb. Shut the door to the cabinet and returned to the kitchen for more chopping. I said nothing to anybody about what I had found. I didn't want to nark on my brother.

The skeleton was next. It hung suspended from the garage ceiling, unpolished, yellowing. It looked brittle. By this time, my mother was fairly resigned. Rather than berating her son about the strange objects, all now inanimate, all once animate, she chose to ignore the skeleton, the brain, the heart, to act as if nothing unusual was going on in our household. Being angry or upset, she reasoned, would only egg him on. Better to shrug it off, make another pot of fig jam, do a bit more cleaning, to act, most convincingly, as if she was not in the least disturbed by this odd accumulation of organs and bones that gathered about our home; this strange invasion.

My usual route home from school was along the Railway Reserve. This was an uninhabited stretch of land that, as the name would suggest, had been set aside in order that train tracks, running from the coast to our town, might one day be put there. The tracks had never been laid; they'd got some two hundred miles inland before deciding that supplies and passengers were better off hitting the road, but the reserve remained, like some weird reminder of all that could have been but never was. I liked the reserve, the long grass that reached up to my knees, the insects that hopped and buzzed about, the solitude. From a distance it looked like a cornfield. I was thirteen, on the verge of adolescence. I needed my time alone. Like my brother, I was an odd boy. *Different*, said my mother. But everybody knew what she meant. One of my favourite pastimes was throwing frogs against the garage wall and watching them splatter.

When I wasn't alone, I was often with my friend Vincent, who was considered unusual because of his flaming red hair. It took so little, to set you apart, to mark you out for ostracism. On my first day at high school, I'd saved Vincent from the impending fate of a 'dunny dunk' by giving one of the beefy fourth formers who held him a boot in the shins, and delivering a mean right hook to the nose of the other boy, who'd had the intended victim's arm pushed up behind his back. The previous summer, my brother had given me boxing lessons; he said I needed to know how to defend myself. He taught me how to make a fist, fingers tightly curled, thumb safely tucked in behind the knuckles. He taught me how to jab, how to dance lightly on my feet, how to feint. How to float like a butterfly and sting like a bee. And about the forgotten arm. I didn't get angry often, but when I did, I was wild, like a pit bull on heat. There was nothing like mindless bullying to throw me into a rage. After I had punched and kicked and saved him, Vincent and I were bonded, tight. We pricked our fingers with a needle, rubbed them together, and swore to be blood brothers.

Although I liked Vincent's company, I sometimes needed to get away from him as well. He could be overbearing, clingy. At times I felt like he was smothering me. He would get jealous if I began forming friendships with other boys, would get in a huff and refuse to talk to me until I turned my attention, my efforts, back to him. This put me in a precarious position, as he was often sick with flu or migraine, and on those days, I was either forced to sit alone at lunch time and during breaks, or else, to try and approach some other group of boys, some clique, who always had their own rules, their own social codes, from which I was inevitably excluded. These days were torture and in order to make them more bearable, and to get some breathing space away from Vincent, I had begun to form a friendship with another boy, called Kyle. This union was based largely on a shared thrill gained from harming or destroying various creatures in the animal kingdom, from the great to the small. Kyle had a BB gun and a Swiss army knife that his uncle had given him for Christmas. The knife had a razor-sharp blade. We paralysed pigeons, maimed mice, crippled squirrels. One Sunday we took out the eye of an urban fox. Vincent was too soft for these games. He'd once started crying after I'd wounded the neighbour's cat with a slingshot. Kyle lived just around the corner from me; Vince's house was on the other side of town.

I loved wilderness; Vincent was a born suburbanite. One afternoon, he dragged me to see the new shopping mall that had just been constructed about a mile from our school.

"C'mon," he said. "They've got McDonalds in there and everything. I'll buy you a Big Mac."

I had never eaten McDonalds before and, because such food was forbidden in our household, it held a magical allure for me; the golden arches took on all the mystical grandeur of the gates of heaven itself. I didn't need much convincing. Vince and I walked silently, side by side, towards our destination.

When we arrived we made a beeline straight for McDonalds, and then headed for the centre of the mall where we leant nonchalantly against a wall, devouring our bounty. I was halfway through my burger when Vincent's arm shot out and pointed at a moving object in the near distance.

"Hey," he said, through a mouthful of Filet-O-Fish. "Check out the dumb guy in a bear suit."

Outside Toys 'R Us, to the tune of the Macarena, a bear danced alone. I knew exactly who it was in there, under all that fur, but I said nothing, just stared and continued stuffing my face. Nobody was paying David much attention; I assumed that either the mall or the toy store was employing him to entertain the after school crowds, but maybe I was wrong, maybe he was just amusing himself. Letting off steam. When the music finished he sat down on a nearby bench, removed the head of his suit and muttered to nobody in particular, "I used to want to be a doctor before I became a dancing bear."

Used to? I skulked back in the McDonalds doorway, terrified that he would see me and drag me into his pit of shame.

Vince nudged me hard in the ribs.

"Isn't that your brother?"

"Dunno. Don't think so. C'mon, let's get out of here."

I started walking away without him, knowing that he would follow.

I walked Vincent to his house, then doubled back on myself and meandered along the reserve for a while. This place had always felt like a sanctuary, now it felt desolate, empty, like a deserted children's playground. David had always wanted to be a doctor. As kids, I'd been his willing patient, stretching myself out on the kitchen table, pretending to be etherised while he prodded about, examining me, solemnly pronouncing tragic diagnoses. I never had more than days to live. I knew that he must've been kicked out of med school; I couldn't imagine him leaving voluntarily. Seeing him in his bear suit had disturbed me. Was this what adult-hood had in store, this failure of dreams and ambition, this humiliation, this fall from grace?

That evening, I knocked on the door to David's room. When he didn't answer, I pushed open the door and entered anyway. He was lying on his bed, staring at the ceiling. I sat down on the end of his bed and picked at the bedspread, which was navy blue, covered in loops you could pull, unravel. The blades of the ceiling fan overhead spun slowly, softly, *whoosh, whoosh, whoosh.* Several books on alternative medicine graced his bookshelves.

"I saw you in the mall this afternoon," I said, after a spell.

"I know," he replied. "I saw you leaving."

There was a ten second pause that seemed as if it might open up and swallow us.

"I've been kicked out," he said eventually.

This time it was my turn to say, "I know."

"Wanna know why?"

"Of course."

His shoulders started shaking, though I was unsure whether this was with mirth, or some other emotion.

"Well, they have this head box, which is where they put the heads of cadavers after they've been severed from their bodies. Anyway, for a joke, I hooked up a mechanical laughing device, so that whenever you opened up the lid, you'd get this hideous cackling. Guess the dean of the school didn't see the funny side of it."

"Harsh."

"Yeah, everybody said how unfair it was."

Could you really be kicked out, just for that? Was

he lying or telling the truth? Maybe he had done something else, something far worse. Maybe he had just got bored and quit.

"So what do you need those bits of bodies for now then?" I questioned. "All that stuff kind of creeps me out."

"Oh those. I've been nicking them. Don't tell Mum. She'd have a fit."

"Nicking them?"

"The dumb-arses forgot to take my swipe card back, so I've been sneaking past the security guard at night, getting into the labs and stealing shit. Whatever I can lay my hands on."

"But you've left now. You don't need that stuff anymore."

"I thought that maybe I could be, y'know, a self-taught doctor."

"What? Don't be stupid. You need the training, the qualification. They'll take you back, Dave. They can't kick you out just for that."

"Oh, but they can though. They did. I don't care. In the meantime, I can earn some extra cash with the bear thing."

"Are you going to tell them?"

"Tell who?"

"Mum and Dad. You can't just keep pretending that you're still at med school forever."

"Yeah," he said. "One day. When I think they're ready."

He rolled over onto his stomach and turned his face into the pillow. I knew it was my cue to leave.

I trudged around to Kyle's house. We mucked about outside for a couple of hours, taunting the neighbour's

Alsatian with a piece of steak on the end of a barbeque fork, dangling it over the fence, then yanking it back when he lunged for it, hosing down the cat with the water blaster that Kyle's dad had been using on the house, destroying every spider web we could find. When it grew too dark to see I told Kyle that it was time for me to go home.

"Hey," he said, as I was leaving. "I almost forgot what I was going to tell you. Yesterday morning I woke up early and I saw this bird, rare, you know, in the tree outside my window. Bright blue and yellow feathers. Looked like some kind of parrot."

"Wow," I said. "Weird. Maybe somebody's pet escaped."

"It was there again this morning, too. Like some kind of gaudy crow. Showing off, you know. Asking for it."

I laughed.

"Yeah. Show-off."

"So, anyway, if you get here tomorrow morning, early, before school, maybe we can get it with the BB gun. Just wound it. Stun it a little. Then we can examine it up close. Maybe it's never been seen before. Maybe we will have discovered a new species. You get money for that, you know. And fame."

He posed against the wall, a triumphant hunter, holding an imaginary bird by one scaly leg, hand on hip, chin at a jaunty angle.

"You're on," I said.

"Six-thirty."

"I'll set my alarm."

I awoke with the dawn, and made my way to my friend's house. One by one, the streetlights flickered off, as if the darkness was something contagious each lamp passed along to the next in line. Kyle was standing outside his house with his BB gun. As I approached he put his finger to his lips and pointed up at the shape in the tree. The bird looked enormous, out of place, a gigantic multi-coloured albatross. I had never seen anything like it in my life. Kyle took aim and fired. The pellet hit the bird squarely in the chest, right where its heart would be. It squawked once, then fell from the tree and landed with a solid thud at our feet.

"Holy shit," said Kyle. "It looks even bigger now. It's massive."

I was filled with a sudden panic.

"I think we've killed it. What if this bird's the last of its kind? Won't we get in trouble?"

"In trouble with who? Nobody's ever seen it except for you and me. Nobody else knows anything about it."

He plucked a feather from its plumage, and whistled long and low.

"Phew! Look at the size of that momma! Go on, Larry. Get plucking."

The bird looked so helpless, so defenceless, so dead. I felt nauseous, like I had been on a long, winding journey in the hot sun, in a car with all the windows wound up. But I couldn't risk Kyle thinking that I was soft, that I wasn't a man. I reached down and took two feathers, gave him the V-sign with them, then threw them scornfully to the ground. Not to be beaten, Kyle got to his knees and ripped two handfuls of plumage from the bird, laughed at me, or at something, and then stuffed the feathers down the front of his pants, like a codpiece. It was a competition now. I got down beside him and began pulling out great chunks of feathers, throwing them all around us, like the corny pillow ads I had seen on TV at other people's houses. The bird was still warm, like undercooked meat. Part of me wanted it to protest, to rise up against us, peck at our eyes and tear at our clothes, but it couldn't, of course, it couldn't. When we were done, we fell about laughing, keeling against one another like ships that had lost their ballast. The remains of the bird lay beneath the tree, plucked, like a chicken. When Kyle wasn't looking, I picked up a single blue feather and put it in my pocket.

The two of us walked to school and entered the classroom together, still laughing about the dumb bird. My right hand was in my pocket, wrapped around the quill of the feather. Vince was sitting by himself, arms folded, staring blankly into space. He was quiet for a moment, then got up from his chair and walked across to address Kyle.

"Did you know, *Mr Kyle,* that Larry's brother is a bear, a dancing bear."

Spit flew from his mouth as he pronounced the word *bear.*

"He's not a med student at all. He's a bear, a dumb *bear.*"

He began ape-ing about the classroom, humming the Macarena.

"Ehhhhhh Macarena."

Truth be told, I wasn't in the mood for it.

"Shut the fuck up, Vince." I said. "Shut the fuck up."

"Larry your family is *weird.* Rabbit food and no TV. No wonder you wound up *freaks.*"

"I'm telling you to shut your gob, you Mummy's boy, you faggot."

"Faggot? Who're you calling faggot, Kyle lover.

175

Kyle, wanna come kill some pigeons? Kyle, wanna rip the hind legs off a cat?"

Something exploded near the front of my head. I lunged at him, grabbed him by the collar and shoved him against the wall.

"Shut your fucking face, or I'll shut it for you."

"Kyle wanna come suck my cock?"

That was when I left him have it, socked him one, full in the face. His head hit the wall behind him with a thwack, and then he slumped down on the ground, out cold. Out for the count. His nose hung crooked, broken, on his face. I was sent to the headmaster's office. Severely reprimanded. Threatened with suspension and given three detentions.

At home, something else had been broken; the news. My mother was furious. She'd gathered up all David's medical textbooks, the heart, the brain, the bones and thrown the lot out onto the street. She'd kicked my brother out also, shoved him through the door and told him to go and get himself a proper job, and somewhere else to live, she wasn't going to pay for his food, his clothes, his electricity, if he wasn't going to toe the line. He'd been caught sneaking into the department at night. The school dean had rung her up and told her the whole sorry story.

"And the *worst* part is," she was yelling, as I turned into the driveway, "the very worst part is that you lied to me. You deceived me. Pretending to be a part-time bear, when really you were full-time and had nothing else to do, nowhere else to go."

When David saw me, he just shrugged his shoulders, plucked a pair of jeans and a T-shirt from his belongings that were out on the street, gave us all a small wave and trudged off into the distance. God only knew where he was going.

That night I dreamt that the bird was at my window, featherless. You could see its skeleton through its skin.

"I'm sorry," I said. "I'm sorry."

But the bird just shook its head sorrowfully from side to side and tears like blue jewels fell from its eyes. And I knew that what had been done was done, and could never be undone or forgotten.

Shakti Bhatt

Born Again

Saro was a rebel even at ten. Her mother put her in an Irish convent where, daily, their 30-minute morning prayers ended with three Hail Mary's. She didn't say it. She belonged to the Marthomite Church; they were followers of St. Thomas and their only god, her father said to her every night, was Jesus.

She's been in the car for over an hour and the dry heat and dirty air are getting to her. If she does not reach there on time the fights with her husband will have been in vain. She missed the first prayer session in Bombay, and she couldn't, she had reminded herself for the last three months, miss this one. She got here on an overnight train, Cochin to Bangalore, eight hours. She had to ask her nephew to drop her to the station.

She is in her cousin's car, the cousin who stopped speaking to her six years ago. Ever since she announced it. When they were growing up, she was his favorite, that's what he told her. He liked her for not disappearing into the kitchen when she came for holidays. He liked her stories of the village, of the latest prank she had played. He'd even convinced her to wear pants at a wedding, for which he'd taken a beating from his mother. From his first trip abroad—to work with a radio station in Pennsylvania—he brought her a purse made of semi-precious stones, a tiny purse with a thin silver string. In a note inside, he wrote: For the most independent girl I know.

The car is inching forward.

"This is like driving in Bombay," she tells the driver.

"Yes."

"I read in the paper that breathing this city air for a day is like smoking 47 cigarettes."

"Yes."

"Such a thick, smelly air. Why don't they have CNG here, like in Delhi? Have you been to Delhi?"

"No. But my father's brother's son has."

"Roll up your windows a little bit. No, not that much, yes, that's fine."

"I will put on a/c?"

"No, don't bother. These Maruti engines can hardly take it. I don't know why my cousin's office does not give him a bigger car. You cannot even accelerate properly. I know. I used to drive one in Bombay."

"Yes madam. Everything you say is true."

"And a/c uses much too much petrol."

"Yes."

She was married at 20. She was in the last year of college, studying subjects she had little interest in, spending most of her time watching Rajesh Khanna's romances and thinking about marriage. Will her husband be the dutiful pilot of *Aradhana* or the irrepressible comic of *Anand*? A sister-in-law suggested her youngest brother—he had just returned from Delhi with an engineering degree—as a prospective son-in-law. Saro had, of course, seen him at the wedding. He grinned at all the girls and once when no one was looking pinched her cheeks hard. Without losing a moment, she took his hand and twisted it as far as she could.

A meeting was arranged. They were Jacobites, or Yacobis as her family called them, and though a Marthomite would have been ideal, her mother asked her to 'be open about these things'. When the car arrived, four men and a pregnant woman stepped out. He was not one among them. His older brother said there wasn't room enough for him. The expecting woman was his brother's wife and the three other men were his father, his younger brother, and a cousin. Only the older brother talked. He asked her if she had read any books. Then he asked her a few questions about Shakespeare ("Do you think Lady Macbeth was mad or misunderstood?"). The others ate fried banana and lentils. After they left, her cousin—in town for the meeting—said she was lucky to be marrying into such a family: the older brother had run twice for the village assembly. So what if he had failed? He had translated all the works of a French poet into Malayalam; he was also the only person in his village to keep a bidet.

The car—arranged despite her cousin's wish by his wife—trails a Tata SUV, on whose back a sticker says, 'My master is a Jewish carpenter.' The road to the right is practically empty. A few rickshaws and single-passenger cars drive past a large billboard that asks Benly Hyne to 'go back to America.' It calls him 'America's False Prophet' and says 'Hindus Oppose Religious Conversion.' At the bottom is his picture defiled with black paint. She tries not to be dismayed. *People of God are always misunderstood.*

She thought herself lucky to meet her husband before the wedding. A phone call was made by the mother of the groom-to-be apologising for her son's desire to see his wife before the wedding. He drove an Ambassador to her house. He brought two friends with him. They were to go for a drive; she would be accompanied by her sister. They sat in the back with one of his friends. Ten minutes into the drive he stopped the car outside a sweets stall and asked his other friend to move to the back. He looked at her and grinned. She moved to the front and soon after he caught her right hand and squeezed it. She twisted it gently and they laughed in silence. He reminded her of the rough boys she used to play catch-the-thief with. She would always be the cop; she was the fastest runner amongst them. She'd count up to ten with her eyes closed (she never cheated). The boys ran in all directions to hide. Most of them climbed the mango trees around her courtyard. She'd climb each tree in the knee-length handsewn cotton dresses her mother made and touch the thief, who would trail her to catch the others. Many years later, when she met one of the boys at a cinema, he told her that they hid in the trees to catch a glimpse of her panties. The boy who saw it the most number of times received the biggest share of stolen mangoes from her father's trees.

The car reaches the airfield around which there are only stray shops and a few low buildings under construction. The city has been left far behind. There are numerous gates through which people are passing in waxing numbers. She goes inside and counts 26 giant gray cloth screens spread evenly across the field on three sides. The screens are placed in the middle of large squares separated by wooden poles; in each of these areas are rows of green, blue, and red chairs.

She has a VVIP pass folded several times over in her palm-sized clutch. The ticket was given to her by her church, the Good News Chapel. But those seats look like they were filled some time ago, the people comfortable, deriving satisfaction from looking at other people scurrying for seats. The much bigger VIP sections behind them are packed as well, with barely a few empty seats though there is still an hour for the prayer to begin. Her sister-in-law told her that someone gave her cousin a VVVIP pass and he had declined. She cursed him now, asked Jesus to forgive her for cursing, and found a seat in the general section.

She could hardly see the stage from where she was. She could only make out a black rectangular spot surrounded by pools of color—which, when the screens were activated, turned out to be flower pots. The vertical silver line dividing the horizontal darkness would become the podium. Ascending on steps behind the stage are 2500 choir singers from across the country; they have been in the city rehearsing for a month. She knows this because the daughter of her friend is one of them. The daughter is from Delhi, a computer programmer for Intel. She wants to point her out, but to the right stranger at the right time.

After her marriage, she moved to Kenya where her husband found work as an engineer. She did not mind moving to Africa. Her only worry was whether she would be able to cook their staple beef fry and pork curry. She had heard many stories about his appetite before marriage. He was a slim man with no more than a few extra inches to his waist but he ate like an elephant. He started the day with six eggs, sometimes more. He would have them with leftover curries from the night before. For lunch he liked four or five black pomfrets with the usual rice and sambar. Dinner was either beef or pork with chicken curry and appams. He was also fond of lamb's liver twice a week. She had learnt all the recipes from her mother but had to unlearn them while training under her mother-in-law. The proportions of tamarind paste (much more), curry leaves (only for show), mustard seed (in everything), onions (don't waste the outer skin), ground coconut (grated freshly, not frozen), and green chilli (cut in fine circles) made it an altogether different cuisine.

"Don't waste your time in cooking," her cousin said when she made him a meal for the first time. Saro looked at his wife, who was trying not to look bitter.

"But it is wonderful to cook for my husband. He is happiest when he is eating. I feel like I am Rajesh Khanna in *Bawarchi*."

"Hindi movies are fantasy. Your life is real, make something of it."

She had two kitchen helpers in Nairobi, experts in goat butchering, who ignored her requests for pig. After eight years of cooking, cleaning, and going for a monthly weekend to the beach, they returned to India. Their first girl—she was six then—was born with developmental problems and the doctors said she would be more comfortable in her own community.

The sun is beginning to disappear. The clean colors—a bright ball of orange against a clean blue sky—remind her of the drawings her daughters made when they were in school. The moon, fully formed, is visible too and is occasionally obscured by facetious clouds on its steady journey. Above her, two helicopters are headed towards the stage. She hears someone say it is

Benly Hyne. She looks around: dark women with double chins wearing chunky gold are walking in saris of all colors and fabric; their hair is pinned with the strong-scented white jasmine, red jasmine—prettier but with no smell, and marigolds. There are men with dark, curly hair and unclean sideburns that reach their chin; men with moustaches curved upward and downward; men eating banana chips.

A woman asks her to straighten her legs so her family can pass. Saro had put her legs up so her knees wouldn't hurt. The woman's son tugs at her bloated shoulder bag to get something from inside it. She asks him to wait till they find seats. When the boy continues to pull at the bursting satchel she turns around and slaps him across his cheek, making the clean sound of a single clap. The boy looks around to measure the extent of his dishonor, and for a few moments pretends to look shocked. His expression then changes into one of genuine irritation. He walks on, covering his agitated cheek with his hand, saying, "Come on, mama, just give me the biscuits."

Organizing her pallu thrown askew by the breeze, a frail woman in a yellow sari with a long, unkempt plait hands out prayer request cards. Saro takes a handful and looks for her diary to get the addresses of those who have asked her to pray for them and those for whom she'd like to pray anyway (even if they have asked her not to). She starts to fill the cards: one for partial blindness, one for Hepatitis C, one for an underdeveloped child, one for a husband (for her niece, a Buddhist in her forties), two for barrenness, and two for mercy: one towards a non-believer and the other towards her friend's daughter who had an abortion. She finishes filling out the cards just as the pastor of Karnataka is done with his speech and Benly Hyne comes on stage, taking big powerful steps.

People rise to applaud; she does too. The sound reverberates as if they are all in a cave. She wonders how many people there are around her. Hyne's freshly cut hair shakes with vigor as he jumps on the stage, bows, and greets everyone. He's wearing a white suit with gold buttons. He calls on politicians of different faiths who have been invited to the event—Hindus, Muslims, Sikhs, even Catholics. They slowly file on stage. He introduces each one, places two fingers on their shoulders and says, "Jesus loves you." One of them, Hindu, balding, clad a kurta and dhoti, India's eleventh prime minister who kept his job for less than a year, bends over to touch the evangelist's feet.

The closest screen is to her right. To look at it she has to turn her head a considerable amount. Another, at a more comfortable angle, is located further away.

"Strange to watch a screen at a live event," she says aloud, embarrassed.

"This is, like, Woodstock," a voice from somewhere behind her says.

"What is that?" she wants to ask but checks herself.

Twenty years into her marriage, Saro and her husband were parents to four teenage girls. Her father-in-law was disappointed but he did not say anything except when he mixed toddy and rum.

"Family name," he would tell his nieces and nephews. "It is all we have. It is disappearing."

They tried a fifth time but it was a miscarriage—the dead child was a girl.

They raised their daughters in Bombay. The city had a good school for the eldest daughter who at nineteen could not visit the bathroom on her own. The youngest was interested in dance and the other two were studying business, their marriage an anxious presence in their parents' minds. During that time, a friend who lived nearby came to visit them in East Bandra. The friend came on a Sunday morning wearing a plain brown sari and no jewelry, and asked if she wanted to accompany her to her church. She knew about born again Christians, had heard many bad things from her husband. But she recalled her mother's advice to be open, her cousin's motto of independence.

The church was called the Best Blessing Chapel; it was a small white block building with one door and no windows. Inside, a high, unadorned ceiling matched the floor that had no benches in sparseness. Slim steps joined the two sides of the building and led to another unremarkable space where a choir of more than a couple of dozen people stood, men and women on the same side. A small, hardly noticeable statue of Christ on a wooden cross hung on a pillar, which was constructed in the middle of the raised platform and painted the color of dull sky. The choir songs were like nothing she had heard before. The choir of her Marthomite church was ridiculed by parents and children alike for the somnolence of its delivery. The voices and the words she heard at Best Blessing seemed to come from somewhere else; they were united, loving, believing. They weren't doing this because they had to; they wanted to. People around her raised their hands, and moved from side to side. Their eyes were closed, brows furrowed, and they were singing, "Jesus, O my Jesus, till our minds. Fill our hearts with love and forgiveness."

"...Jesus O my Jesus, discharge your mercy upon us sinners. Till our minds..." People around her get up from their seats and sway to the combined echo of

2500 voices. Saro stands as well; her hips shaking lightly as her knees move back and forth in rhythm to the song. A man behind her whom she noticed earlier for his loud voice is not singing along with the choir but providing background harmonies combined with energetic physical movement. Another man to his left who has tied a cloth over his hand and has tears streaming down his closed eyes is singing the song in Kannada. The only person sitting is a pregnant woman, her head bent, shoulders moving with the beat. Hyne asks people to clap: three times, then once. Clap-clap-clap, a clap, clap-clap-clap, a clap. It goes on long enough to lose that instinctive, and consequently short-lived, voluntary spirit. Hyne asks them to stop.

"Lord, we are thankful to you for protecting us," Hyne says, holding a red leather Bible so big Saro can see it without looking at the screen. "Rest our country Bharatmata, our city Bangalore, our state Karnataka in peace. Fill the two million people here with your love, kindness and forgiveness. We are hungry for..." She realizes she has not eaten since lunch. She sits and unwraps the tomato and cucumber sandwiches with coriander dip and spicy tomato sauce that her sister-in-law packed for her. She is ashamed; no one around her is eating. But she has to eat. It was the only thing her husband had said the day she left: "Take your meals on time." It is suddenly quiet and she thinks everyone is looking at her. She takes a bite only when she is sure no one's looking and chews only when someone speaks on the microphone or claps in the audience. The rest of the time she keeps the food, already soggy, clogged in her mouth.

It is getting dark. Above her, the moon is almost full. The sun has left an orange screen in the sky, which splits into darker shades away from the horizon. The wind has become steady; it raises the hair on her arms and she wishes she'd brought her shawl.

The pastor calls upon God to heal his ailing children. She wonders what God thinks about cancer, about AIDS.

"My friends, my brothers and sisters," Hyne says, "Jesus, our father, our king is asking you that same question—will thou be made whole?"

"Yes," Saro shouts with the others.

"Will thou be made whole?" He is bending, his back parallel to the ground.

Yes, they shout again. Everyone is standing, some are shaking with fresh tears. Next to her is a woman who has covered her head with her sari and holds a son in a fleece suit against her shoulder. He looks around him with eyes wide open, at the figures, their movements, their noise. He starts to cry.

Hyne starts the roll call: "Bleeding of nose, fibrosis, brain tumor, muscular dystrophy, tumor in the uterus, loss of speech, deafness, diabetes...Call his name with your body and with your soul and a miracle will happen."

A miracle happened for me. Saro thanks the Lord, joining her hands over her head and bowing. It was two years ago when her husband had a heart attack. For a couple of days he had been complaining of a chest pain. She gave him Nimdone but the pain grew worse. At the time they were living in his family home, in Kerala, more than three hours away from her father's house. After her first visit to the Best Blessing Chapel in Bombay, she began going every week with her friend.

"Dear Lord," Saro prayed, "free me from my duties by the year 2000 and I will serve you for the rest of my life." That year her father-in-law died and left each son 18 acres. She decided to grow commercial rubber and coconut trees on their share. In the next five years all her daughters were married, in order. The oldest one found a match in Pune, a 25-year-old boy who lived with his father and his aunt, and had a live-in therapist. The couple moved to the family home, where no one was willing to move because it was on a small island surrounded by a big river full of white fish and water spiders. In her husband's village she began to volunteer at the Good News Chapel twice a week. Her husband was against it but she had found her calling. He had stopped working as soon as he got his inheritance, selling off a few dozen coconuts and mangos without her knowledge.

"I am sick of your activities," he said, the meat and alcohol in his body raging. "Why are you doing this foolish religious business?"

"It is not foolish. You are ungrateful. You think it was because of you that our daughters got married? Did you get us these 18 acres?"

"So what. It's because of my family that we live here and we get food to eat. Those families married their sons to our daughters because they knew about my father. He was the first.."

"The first person in the village to get a bidet. Nobody knows what a bidet is and nobody cares. You must not be so ungrateful to the Lord."

"What lord shord. I am your lord. Come here, I'll show you how grateful I am."

"You better start believing otherwise when the day comes, the day of…"

"Enough with this nonsense. You can do what you want, don't tell me about it. I will throw you out of the house."

"Like you can live without me even for a day," she said, not looking up from the church invites she was collecting from her printer. "When the day comes, it is my prayers that will save your life."

When the pain persisted for two days, she asked her friend to take them to the hospital. Her brother-in-law was only a few minutes away but they weren't on talking terms: he thought they received a larger share of the property then he; he started to plant palm trees on their land and when he did not stop they went to court. That was six years ago; they had still not had a hearing. In the car, on the way to the hospital, Saro sat in the back with her husband, his head on her shoulders. She was rubbing his back with one hand and holding his chest with another, his hand over hers.

"Give me a sign of assurance," she prayed, "something that will tell me everything will be fine." A few moments later she saw a tourist bus pass by.

"Praise the Lord," she said aloud and crossed herself.

"Why are you thanking God? Has he died?" her cousin said.

"Dirty mouth you have. Did you see the bus that just passed by?"

"Yes."

"Did you see what it said?"

"What did it say?"

"It said Cherian."

"That's why you're thanking the Lord?"

"Never mind, you fool, just keep driving."

It was her husband's family name. She knew her husband would be fine.

Laura Heggie

Avoiding the Issue

It's six p.m., the beginning of the danger zone. I've decided that it's best if I don't go out at six. Things are clearer at half-eight-ish; the rules of place return. Anyway, the point is, by nine it's always safe to go to the office.

I've been meeting Ben here for a little while now, maybe six months. Nothing to get excited about. Which is to say, I'm not excited. He is.

*

"Of course I think they'd probably prefer it if you just sat down and had a chat with them, y'know Cass. I think it's *company* that they need."

Ben is in preaching mode.

"I mean maybe if you just *talked* to them for a bit, got to *know* them, you wouldn't have to keep running away from them."

"I don't run away from them."

"Cass, I've seen the map. It's so childish."

"Yes well, then you're a *paedophile*, aren't you?"

That wasn't really a good comeback in hindsight. My debating skills are taking a nosedive. I decide to cut my losses and go for a straightforward ultimatum:

"Here or nowhere."

Ben and I arrange another meeting for Tuesday. I like to keep my weekends free for girlfriends and potentials. Things haven't quite worked out the way I planned with Ben. I think weekday evenings are the right place for him. He is marginally better than 'Eastenders': our meetings are stupid, depressing and shouldn't happen in real life, but they are compulsive. And Ben definitely has the edge, because you don't have to commit to four nights a week.

I'm in a worse mood than normal, mainly because Ben has been a little too obvious during office hours recently. He thinks he's being subtle. You see, last week we acquired an 'intern', which essentially means an office junior who they don't have to pay. His name is Ed. Ed's OK. He looks a bit scruffy, kind of like a school rebel. Ben is Ed's overall manager, but I'm supposed to 'task' Ed; which essentially means I hand him pieces of paper to photocopy. I am also supposed to 'mentor' him, which essentially means I go to the park and eat M&S sandwiches with him two lunchtimes a week. Which is fun, because teaching him the ways of the workplace means that we can bitch about everyone.

Ben has decided that he should make Ed feel at home, he does this by constantly interrupting our conversations with irritating quips like "She's not working you too hard is she? I've heard Cassie can be quite a taskmaster," and asking Ed whether he's settling in ok. When we're out at lunch, Ed makes up little nicknames for people; he calls Ben 'The Niceman'. When Ed sees him coming over to interrupt our conversations he winks and says 'the Niceman cometh'.

In fact, it's Ben's niceness that I hate. It's as if he can't even compute anything that isn't completely right-on, left-leaning or middle of the road. He refuses to believe that *they* have a victim system, even though I've explained it all. It's a simple idea: if we're walking down the street and I am victim-side, any Sitters we pass will concentrate on me. A good gentleman, or boyfriend, or partner, or whatever will know to swap places with a lady who is victim-side. I have tried explaining this to Ben, but he doesn't understand. You see, if Ben is victim-side, he immediately gives money to his assailant. Which then leads the aforementioned assailant to ask his partner – namely me – whether I can 'spare any change' as well? And if they do that and you say no, then the bastard has humiliated you in front of your boyfriend, or colleague, or whatever. In fact, you are even worse than those people who walked past and ignored him in the first place. So basically you can't win with Ben, you either have to take victim-side or be put on the spot. Which is why I've given up walking anywhere with him.

*

On Tuesday, Ben is in a 'romantic' mood because he's brought along candles and he's saying things in a soft voice. He has a couple of saucers to catch wax drips and an obviously pre-prepared speech for the occasion.

"Cass,"

He's tipped his head to the side a bit to prove that he *really does care.*

"Happy six month anniversary! I've been thinking. About us. I think we should take this thing to the next level."

"Well, I don't think I'm ready for anal, Ben."

Oh God, I've been spending too much time with Ed. This isn't the time to be a smart-arse; especially as whatever he's about to ask, I'm pretty sure the answer is going to be 'No'. Unless he miraculously comes out with "You know Cassie, the way I see it, I should continue to adore you, whilst you should be completely free to do what you want, not return my calls, see other men and not feel guilty if one day you just want to leave me without any explanation."

Unfortunately it transpires that the 'next level' doesn't quite fall within these parameters. But I'm on relatively good form this time, and manage to deflect all suggestions of telling our friends, going on holiday together, and even going to dinner in town. Well done me. However, I do have to make one concession. I have to talk to a homeless person, and be nice.

*

The challenge is tough, but I'm going to give myself a few breaks. I'm lucky, I have the map, and it's still accurate, despite the fact that I drew it up four years ago when I first moved to Bristol. To be honest, there are actually two maps; one pre-six and one post-half eight. Before six they are in shopping areas, and after half eight, they have moved nearer to the pubs and clubs. In between there is no rule of place, which is why I call it the danger zone.

I think it's very important that for this particular encounter I find myself a Sitter, which is why I'm using the maps. You see, there are two species of homeless: The Sitters and the Walkers. In Bristol we have both. In smaller towns you only get Sitters; Big Issue sellers are included in that group. The basic idea is that they stick to one patch, and only move within a two-metre radius of that patch. If they move outside this radius it's their lunch break or something. They're sort of like those people who won't talk about work after they've got home. Except they don't have a home. But anyway, the point is, outside their particular spot they can't harass you. Life would be a lot better if the world only contained Sitters. Everyone could just buy a map with all their locations on it, and plot their routes around that. Kind of like the way everyone tries to avoid the M25. Now Walkers, they're the real insidious bastards.

It's the guilt you see, the homeless are evolving, they're becoming more savvy. They know how the population is split. They know that there are reluctant altruists who wouldn't give to them if they were easily avoidable. At first they thought they could catch these people as Sitters. That was when they developed the cunning ploy of having one Big Issue seller on each side of the road. That way when you cross the street to avoid one, you immediately bump into another, your guilt overwhelms you and you buy it from him. It's a conspiracy. When they saw how effective that was, the Walkers started appearing. In a way we should be grateful for the Walkers, because they've pretty much put a halt to homeless people working together. There's no 'homeless cartel' any more; it's every man for himself. And now that the Walkers are taking over, the people who would give money to Sitters, the "look at me" altruists like Ben, well, by the time they get to the Sitters, they've already given all their money away to Walkers.

So the remaining Sitters all have to go out and become Walkers as well.

However, there are still a few straggling Sitters and I am going to choose one. The most obvious choice is one outside a WH Smith, as this is a prime spot in most places, and should therefore attract a more old-school type of homeless person. But popular places do lend themselves to the 'comedy' homeless; those who try and spice up their act with bad jokes and a jester's hat. No, I want a quiet chat. So it'll have to be Marks and Spencer.

*

I go in one of my free lunch hours. His name is Patrick, and he's originally from Manchester. In the end we have quite a pleasant conversation. He tells me that he's got trench foot from his leaky shoes, I tell him I'd give him mine but kitten heels might make his calves look chunky. He says he wouldn't want to ruin them because they look so good on me. He tells me he had a daughter around my age, but she hasn't spoken to him for five years, and we speculate on what she does now and where she's living. I ask what her name is, and even offer to help find her using the Internet at work. But he says that's ok; she doesn't need to know that her Dad is homeless. And if I really want to do him a favour I should ring my Dad tonight, because he's sure Dad would love to hear from me. I think I will. It's nearly two.

"Well I'd better get back to work then. Nice to talk to you"

"Oh wait, before you go…"

And then he asks me for money. I mean, did everything I said to him just mean nothing? And then it comes to me. The fucking homeless are just like fucking men; you talk to them, you open up, and you think perhaps at last you're forming one of those perfect, meaningful platonic friendships, and then they try to have sex with you. Except the homeless ask for money. Although I'm pretty sure if I'd have stayed there any longer Patrick would have tried for sex as well.

The worst thing about the whole affair is that it's made me even more annoyed with Ben. Because Ben thinks that behaviour like Patrick's is fine. In fact, he seems to like the idea of having a homeless person all his own. So every week he goes and buys the Big Issue from the same bloke; this vile man called Dave. Ben romanticises it, as if he has some incredible loyalty to Dave, as if they're friends. I'm certain that all Dave thinks is 'Not *him* again; I'll have to endure more of his inane conversation before he gives me the money'. In fact, I bet Dave prefers the people who just buy a Big Issue and bugger off.

*

I am mentoring Ed today. This is excellent, and for more than one reason. Firstly, I don't have to make up an excuse not to spend lunchtime with Ben. And secondly, I think Ed's appearance in the office has actually cheered me up quite a bit. Good to know that there's someone in a more pathetically junior position than me, for a change. I think I might mention it to him.

"Ed, do the homeless cheer you up?"

"No."

A homeless guy is coming towards us. Bugger. I hate it when they corner you on benches. But as he spies Ed with me, he thinks better of it. Result. I suppose Ed does look quite tough in a way. He's not acting so jovial today, but I don't mind. Ben looks like an optimist, all floppy fringed and Labrador-like. Ed currently looks like he'd bite the head off a puppy given the opportunity. He's eating a deep-filled chicken sandwich, wrapping his chops around it, noisily chomping away like a lion with a Christian. The sandwich looks delicious. Ed licks his fingers. Low fat yoghurt dressing is dripping from my tikka wrap onto my skirt.

*

The next time I see Ben, it's me who has the prepared speech. I tell him about my encounter with Patrick, and I unveil to him my new Continental-style solution to the problem of homelessness.

"You see Ben, in Spain, they kneel down, staring at the pavement, hanging their heads. When you give them money, it feels as if you're blessing them. The point is it should be easy to walk past them. In that case you're really giving. And you feel happy, not bullied or blackmailed. Nowadays even if you have given to the homeless it doesn't make you feel good, because you've always been pushed into it. When they launched the Big Issue they said it was to give the homeless a sense of pride and a work ethic, and so they wouldn't just feel like people pitied them. But actually it was to make the people buying it feel good. It's proof that you're a socially conscious all-round great person…"

It is at this point that I realise we're not alone in the office. Ed is sitting at my desk looking at some files. He looks up, and for a second I can register terror crossing his face. But then I watch it dawning on Ed that Ben and I are here for pleasure, not business. I watch it dawning on Ben that I bunk off early and give Ed the keys to lock up. I hate being found out. Ed starts smiling and looks at Ben. This is going very well for Ed; not only has his manager just found him working late, but he now has great blackmail material and the ensuing guaranteed excellent reference. Ed is smirking. Ben is smiling too. I'm beginning to think there must be some kind of conspiracy. Ben turns to me and says, "Well, I guess it's all out in the open now" and puts his arm around my shoulders. Wanker! My rhetoric abandons me; I shrug Ben's arm off and run away.

In fact, I'm so distracted on the way home that I fail to recognise a Walker in time:

"Excuse me lady, you couldn't spare any change? I'm trying to get enough together for a bottle of cider."

I give this man every last penny I have on me and walk home feeling exhilarated.

*

The next day Ed is looking pleased with himself, but he doesn't rub it in. He jokingly calls me "The Nice Maiden", but in the grand scheme of things I'm getting away quite lightly. Ben is being a twat and tries to talk to us all through the morning, until Ed finally gets rid of him by saying that if he doesn't have enough to get on with we could always give him some of our filing. At lunchtime, Ed asks me about my new plan for the homeless, and seems really quite interested in what I have to say. I say I hate the homeless and everyone hates the homeless, but they can't admit it to themselves. I tell him about the Shelter poster I saw which says the 'The silent homeless' needed our help, the ones you don't see. Even Shelter knows we all hate the homeless. He says he thinks they all hate us too, and they hate you more if you say something like "No, sorry" when they ask for money than if you just walk past.

"It's like that joke – 'What's the difference between a tart and a bitch?' 'A tart sleeps with everyone, a bitch sleeps with everyone except you'. Ben's a tart, homeless people see him, they know he's easy, they know he's going to give it to them. But when you say 'Sorry,' or 'I haven't got my wallet on me,' then you're a bitch. You've obviously got money, you just think maybe you'd prefer to buy a coffee with it. But instead of just getting on with it and buying a coffee, you're flirting with them."

Eventually I descend into a rant: that guy who wanted to buy cider, that was the truth. That's why I gave him my money. But in a week's time, if it works, that'll just be his line. How long before we're inundated with bloody post-modern homeless people all walking around asking for cash to buy skag? There's a man up by the Texaco garage who carries a petrol can around with him and asks people for money because his car's broken down. No one gives him money for telling the truth, so he's even buying props. Ed reckons that guy should try and get government funding and call what he does 'street theatre'. Ed and I start having a little competition to see who can compose the most pitiable, yet believable homeless speech. Ed's starts "Before you ignore me or turn me away, please listen". I think that's a bit 'door-to-door' salesman for me. I am going to hone my speech to perfection. It is a very intelligent thing to have a good pity speech ready, just in case. Although I'm pretty sure I could make a good living as a whore if it came to that. Ed agrees.

But the fun has to stop. Ed brings up the subject of Ben.

"I thought you hated him?"

"Well, I don't like him much. It all just got a bit out of hand."

"Cassie, he told me you'd been seeing one another for six months!"

I can't explain anything. So I say nothing. The truth is that since I met Ben, everything I've tried to do or say has been the wrong thing. I was trying to be nice, so I didn't laugh in his face when he asked me for a drink. And then I didn't want to reject him because I knew he was a *nice man* so I agreed to see him again. And so on. Ed seems to know what silence means, and stops asking questions.

He bites into his sandwich like it's been teasing him.

"What are you looking at me like that for?"

"Your sandwich. It looks really nice."

"Do you want a bite?"

"If that's ok".

"You shouldn't eat those wraps. They just leave you hungry."

I close my mouth around the sandwich, where Ed has taken a large bite. I taste chicken and lettuce and Ed's saliva. It is a feast.

Ed smiles. He has noticed.

"So, what do you think? Can we maybe meet one night in the office?"

I don't want to soil Ben's territory really.

"I don't know; how many homeless people are there between your place and mine?"

"Just the one".

"Ok great; we'll go to yours then".

"Ok".

"Do you want to write down the address?"

I hand him a compliments slip, and he writes down an address. I'm trying to second-guess him the whole time; I conjure up the map in my head. If there's only one he must live near me, how convenient! In fact the furthest he could live is three miles away. Which is excellent, because I hate public transport.

But it's just the address of the office. Shit. There *is* a conspiracy. Ben's getting revenge. He's told Ed I never let him go anywhere else with me, and now he's trying to make me see how bad he feels. They're working together.

"Actually I'm sort of living there. Temporarily."

Of course, it wasn't exactly what I was expecting. But Ed doesn't say anything more about it, and I know what silence means, so neither do I.

*

Every time my mother goes into town she buys the Big Issue from the first seller she comes to, then walks down the High Street with it under her arm, waving it at the other sellers saying "Sorry, already got one". Sometimes they even shout back things like "good on you madam". But the only reason she bought one in the first place is so they won't bother her. It's like infiltrating the Mafia or something. But this is even better than that; you see Mum's plan has a fatal flaw. Not every homeless person sells the Big Issue, some of them just beg, and if they see you with a Big Issue, they immediately assume that you're a 'look at me' altruist, and they automatically approach you for money. But having Ed there wards them all off, because they know who he is and they know he's trying to fool people and they want to see him succeed, because they think if he does they can too.

Ed lives in the office on a non-temporary basis now. Which is good, because it has a shower. Of course, no one else knows about it, and he has to do an Ann Frank if anyone works late. Luckily he doesn't have many possessions. And no, he's not going to move in with me, because he's still actually homeless, and would probably nick all my stuff. He should be getting a proper job with us soon though. I've let him use my address so he can set up a bank account. Once he has his own flat I think we'll get together properly, provided there aren't too many homeless guys on the way there. We're working on a project as well, Ed is going to be a homelessness mentor, and set up workshops with Shelter to teach non-threatening feel good homeless technique. The first lesson is this: Silence.

Olesya Mishechkina

Charles Magezi-Akiiki/ Daphne Darling

Charles Magezi-Akiiki

1

It's early and cold. Orange construction flowers are in season this time of year. A black guy stretches on the street corner by a flower booth and sneezes. I watch the city lights still aglow from last night. The bums and the seagulls play together in the moonshine. It must be colder outside. How do they sleep like that out in the cold? Drunk as a motherfucker, it's about to rain. The sky is grey, and the pavement is grey. The buildings are grey and gloomy. I want to put out my cigarette on the crying child's head. He must be crying because it is so fucking early and goddamn cold. We pass by the freight trains tagged with graffiti. Some of them are really good. I can barely read what they say. Famous quotes. In oblong, cartoon letters.

There is only one quote I know.

I look out into the parking lot that is a foreground to a city of uneven skyscrapers. It is a cake baking and bubbling bigger in different parts. The electric posts dance in a necklace around them. A good name for a newspaper I saw: The Plebeian.

I smile at the lonely women who buy few groceries and a single cucumber at the store.

Married couples. I will iron your old wife with good conversation.

The old women with crumpled faces and red rouge buy graphic erotica. Pictures of mouths open, and eyes closed. Reminds me of sea lions in aquariums waiting to be fed. The front cover says that he comes in the night. "So what?": her pale shaking hand grabs the book away from me.

Every single product has multitudes of variety with respect to amount, flavor, and quality. We carry 20 different types of cereal, just in the cornflake category. Purple relish. I relish the thought of green ketchup. Individually wrapped finger sausages. Peeled Cactus. Exotic foods from the Far East, bought by people who cannot explain the taste because they speak very little English.

Do not exceed expiration date. Ever.

..

Choice is usually consistent with quality of life. From your choice of foods, it's easy to deduce the number of people you live with, how much money you make per year, the regularity of your stool, and which magazine cover you read last month over the regularity of your stool. Anyone could look at the address on your checks and at the number on your credit card, and claim to be your childhood pal.

Behind a big iron curtain that heeds EMPLOYEES ONLY is where "the magic", as they say, comes into categorical existence. From the outside, the double doors look intimidating. What's behind them? A laboratory of muscular, mutinous rodents with long, drawn out horse-faces, running the spinning wheel to water-power this small, rich, conspicuously clean town? A warehouse-type place, with narrow hallways and stacked catacombs. Resembles a little bit the inside of an airplane or a carwash. Very dark in there. A black, dust-covered power cord behind a neon clown with red eyes that gives children candy for solving arithmetic. Two giant freezer vaults and a room for disposed dairy egging on the stink.

People come out from behind the doors, carefully pulling a small trolley stacked to the ceiling with boxes. Packaged purple relish; green ketchup.

There are people in red coats, and people in blue coats. The people in the red coats carry the weight of spread-sheets recording merchandise coming in and out, as well as spoilt and damaged goods. 200 boxes are stacked each day. The people in the blue coats actually stack the boxes. As Chekov once said, (here it comes) A man never gets tired of looking at the mountains, the ocean, and another man working. In oblong, cartoon letters.

I'm the manager, up front.

Sometimes, one of Donald Duck's sons comes in to supervise. A lord over his fiefdom. He looks over the ecosystem of his living, breathing, pulsing business, still owned by the crazy old man who won't quack. He sits in a small, dark office room, in the corner of the store. It resembles a balcony on a narrow, European street, where clothes are hung on the railing, and plants slowly tilt from side to side with microscopic propinquity.

Narrow stairs lead to the niche. They humble you. They make you watch every step, they creak, and they are never wide enough to hold the entirety of your boot. You resign yourself to the railing. It's a while up. Serious subjects in the back of the mind. Adds to the nervosa. From that veranda, you can see the entire arena of the store, like a cat that likes to sleep in the highest place in the house, so it can both sleep and watch over what is going on in every corner of the room. But from below, only some heads peering out are seen. The shadow in the single office chair is always in a recumbent position; the lackluster and the force of distance blur the particulars of the face and form. You can be certain that they are watching you. Yes, you. And no one else at that particular moment. From the parallax below, you look up at the room. You see talking heads discussing something. They could be heads on a stick; human skin faces, held up by ogres and gnomes that are

Napoleonic in size and fascist in temperament. The victims reach the top at last. Stand up straight. It takes a human being's visage to command others; it can never come from the ogre itself. But once you're up there, your teeth start to itch and you forget about everything. The step ascends from discomfort to humility, to respect, (holding on to the railing) to its sister, fear. So you say what you say as well as you can say it. After it's all over, it is just as difficult descending. The steepness of the exit reserves you to climb down backwards. It's safer to hold on to the railing. You plot one foot down the step, almost bowing to the store director, like a subject that can't turn his back to a Persian king.

2

It would be so easy: Friday evening before the holidays. I can picture it, as I've felt it: A cold evening that leaves people drunk on their feet by the end of the week. The shortening, darkening days that cloud the sun and the streets with brown, red, and yellow leaves. The whirlwinds that occasionally take up a small stack of dry and cracked helpless *curls off the ground, and lazily land a few feet away, as if a burst of inspiration quickly hit and was suddenly forgotten. And they are stiff in their drying as though they died with their mouths open, now having been lodged stiff in place. Yellow ribbons oxidized. Each one the fingerprint of this or that maple, having stood there as long as the old house; sometimes having borne the saga of certain homes; a landmark for drivers and tourists in unfamiliar neighborhoods.* They get off work with the anticipation of a long, carnivorous rest; a fatter stuffing in the gut, a heavier drink, the relaxing, drowsy calm of the stillborn, and the blue, breathless, cold morning of the Sunday, when all the stores are closed and all the churches are open, and a shagging old man waits and smokes in front of a bar a quarter to noon with a fenced-in stampede in his eyes: *down the shot like face hitting pavement. Fuck everything else.* All at once flail from the spells of weekend, forgetting the gnawing anticipation of having to get out of the warm womb of bed, and step with bare feet upon the cold floor of the long day ahead. *It's still dark, and there is so little time to get ready. What a birthing to get out of bed at 5 in the morning. 5 minutes longer and one minute more seem with slip though the cracks. Then, the long piss brewing feelings of perk. Coffee, if there is time. A shit before leaving for the door, because the coffee just kicked in. Shit becoming uncomfortably late. And this feeling makes it go faster.* You turn over sleepishly-sheepishly, flip flopping of flannel and pie crusts of dust in half-closed eyes. It's futile trying to go back to sleep because you forgot to turn off the alarm of death and panic. Thirty minutes later, the eyes won't shut. And it's no good tossing around, for the satisfaction of staying in bed you already have. It is all the less sweet, while the ceiling and the yellow wallpaper do not talk back unless you are insane. Catch yourself in the desultory act of configuring images from the shadows on the walls and patterns in the hardwood. To hell with it! You get up.

Sharon, Kathy, and Andy would close that night: My autistic army. I'd be the last person there; the last man-ager, with one assistant manager.

I'd catch the very next flight somewhere. I'd get away with it. It seems so simple. Why do I tolerate every-thing? Donald Duck's sons are taking away my health benefits so they can afford to break their legs on longer vacations in the Alps.

Sharon and Andy will wash the counters and the floors. Kathy will count the money, and sneak home, because I always let her. From the profit of the day, all the counters that have been open—10 in total— will make a thousand dollars every five hours. Let's see…there are three shifts. That's one, three, six—ok. 30 grand, if I'm lucky. But I never am. That means I will have at least 20 thousand in my pocket. I know how little it is, but I can't help it, I have to do something new. At least it will help me start over, somewhere else. I could teach English. I could drink every day. I do drink every day. I should think of something new to do, to see. Sightseeing. I could travel, finally. Then finish myself off. Like early retirement. I've been here for ten years and I think I deserve it. Or I could do it smart. I'd save the money. I will make it last, I promise. There will be no hotels and no prostitutes, no nightclubs, and no sailboats. I will buy a piece of land, and farm like I used to in my village. I will do it all by the book. I will write a book. I will do *something*.

I can't remain here for the rest of my life—what if I die in this shit? My epitaph planted in rows of thousands: Here lies Charles Magezi-Akiiki. He died in this shit.

I drink whiskey. I draw a bath and I enclose my body in it like a marinade. There is nowhere to go. There is nothing to do. My toes are level with my eyes. I stare at the feet extending from the pelvis, extending from the torso, extending from a part I can no longer see. That is my body. It is not completely old, therefore it's useful. It is useful to others as a means of labor. This long body that barely fits in this concave, sallow, oval piece of ceramic. What of this that I can no longer see? It's useless as a means of labor, anyway. The silence of the bathroom, filled with yellow light, and the reflections of the curtains on the wall. That is my life. Or am I a man sleeping somewhere? No, it couldn't be. Too consistent. (You can go crazy thinking about it) This is my being. I am here in this room, at this moment. Yellow light and bathroom tile. Concave, sallow, oval marinade. There is nowhere to go. There is nothing to see. Because I can't afford it. Because even if I did see something beautiful, I wouldn't be able to recognize it because I'm not interested in its esthetics. I don't understand why people paint pictures that resemble amorphous, obscure shapes, or geometric, uneventful figures. They aren't anything I can recognize from real life, like children in the park, or trees, or animals. Yet they manage to become respected and they earn millions from it. They probably have large bathtubs, so that when they feel like bathing, they can experience the sensations of children swimming in private ponds, and I'm sure they even have those attached back supporters to the side of their tub, so that they don't have to use the back of their occipital bones to support the entirety of their weight. The neck becomes too stiff afterwards. Why are some people lucky like this, but I am not? If I paint a red triangle in the middle of a blank canvas, I won't be taken seriously. People will probably think I'm an idiot and laugh. Anyway, I can't paint at all, I can barely draw. How does fate select these people? Is there a random search, like at the airport? Every millionth person gets a free roundtrip ticket.

Congratulations, you have been chosen to participate in

our promotional offer. Sponsored by Life. The Motto: "Let others live, or at least aspire to live, by your example".

Back on the ground, I am here and there is nowhere to go. And if I slit my wrists, and gorge on the contents of my medicine cabinet, when my blood squirts vacuously into the water, forming abstruse shapes like those of cloud animals in the sky, perhaps only then will I understand all of life's lucky little lottery numbers.

Across the street from my building, men replace the swamp cooler of an expensive restaurant with air conditioning. They drill. It scares the birds away. The windows framed by the thin walls of my apartment shake. I have to listen to it when I come home from work.

Every

single

fucking

day.

I bet they'd kick my ass if I try to say something. They drape the walls with ladders and tear down meandering ivy that gets in the way. They sing in Italian. Italy is so far away. The ivy keeps growing. Sometimes, when I'm soaking in the bath, I can hear the melodies of the songs they sing. They're recognizable, but unnameable. Can't put my finger on it. From an old movie. I don't know the words, so I hum. Perhaps the ivy grows from the carbon dioxide of their vacuous Italian breath. I thought about doing construction. I wouldn't do that kind of work for anything. It's back-breaking. Most of them end up arthritic, broken alcoholics. Lots of problems. Knees, legs, back, arms, joints, headaches. No health insurance. Like old prostitutes. I wonder if they think about that.

3

I can't say that I left my country on good terms. When I applied for citizenship, I didn't know English very well, so I wanted to make sure I knew what I was getting myself into. At that point, being nearly anywhere else would have been better. America was the golden egg; the refreshing zephyr of freedom; the land of, as they say, patriation—an ideal of my country, which in the course of various unpleasant confrontations, had become fruitlessly exhausted, until those who had won made damn sure that those who had lost didn't realize it. America. I was led to a large room that smelled like crammed people, even when it was empty. It was nearly empty, except for one slot that said, IMMIGRATION AND CUSTOMS, where at least fifteen people stood in single file. I was handed blank documents. Everything on the forms was translated. A patient bureaucrat dealt with me in an exchange of exactly three pairs of sentences after a waiting line of several hours. "Name?"

"Charles Magezi-Akiiki"

"Excuse me, what was that?"

I wrote it down. "This. Thank you."

"Please fill out this form and come back. We're closing soon, but you can come back tomorrow. We close at around 4:00, Mon--day through Fri--day," she an-nunciated.

"Thank you very much. Thank you." I smiled at her as though she was in charge of the entire department, granting me approval.

On the form, there were several clauses that claimed citizenship through

the attentively deficient act

of putting a checkmark

in an empty box

next to the articulated choice.

The directions also condemned incorrect markings, as with Xs, or the coloring-in of the belly of the box. Specified ink colors. The choices were written down for me: I claim to be:
[ ] A Family-Sponsored Immigrant
[ ] An Employment-Sponsored Immigrant
[ ] A Diversity Immigrant *(Quicksand!)*
[ ] A Special Category (Specify)_____
...the charge behind the fifth box on the list was as simple as having a million dollars. Unless you're a citizen of Cuba, North Korea, and the entire Middle East, asterisked and listed below this section of the document. I checked the fourth box, specifying Political Asylum.

When I watch Daphne dally carelessly over her counter, I remember my country. How corrupt it is. How girls like her would be eaten alive. All that American femi-

nism. Her thin voice breaking over someone's hand.
Then astounded silence, and the shame that settles like
yellow lamplight in a small one-bedroom apartment
kitchen. You can see their silhouettes behind the curtains, from the street at night. Were they dancing tango?
God forbid she starts to fight back. That's his way of
patronizing. Make sure it tastes good, too. Translated as
survival rather than abuse, intolerance, sexism, and
other academic words. You want to keep your job, talk
to the boss. And all the other girls whisper, *it's her turn
now*. Daphne has no idea. And Sharon? She doesn't
know her own address. *Don't know nothing about nothing*.
Have you ever seen those old fashioned, manual meat
grinders with revolving handles, and a spiral piece on
the inside, which when spun in a certain direction in a
helix, swallows square chunks of meat down like
Charybdis; whose only exit is a round slab of metal with
small holes punched through the entire perimeter? First
the blood squirts out, and then the actual tube of
ground meat, bearing slight resemblance to tightly waving hair in a ponytail. A little bit like that. There
wouldn't be anything left for the birds of Sharon.

America disappointed me. When I lived on the outskirts of the city of K—, I used to watch all the
American action movies with Sylvester Stallone, Steven
Segal, Jean-Claude Van Damme, and Arnold Schwar-
zenegger. The amount of people killed adds up to a
small holocaust. But it was alright because they killed
bad guys, whose maliciousness came from their natures,
which were absolutely and necessarily evil, having no
other motive. They were probably born that way, rip-
ping through their mothers' wombs with coarse, black
facial hair and automatic machine guns. Then they

raped and killed their own mothers. The hero said an idiomatic idiocy, before he shot them between the eyes. He never missed, other than the translation. We all crowded into a small room on a Friday evening, gathering around a television box that was hung on a shelf, in the corner of the room. Farmers working large coffee plantations, in feudal villages. The only joy in life was that movie at the end of the week; like anticipating lambs. There were more people than chairs, so the old ones got to sit first, while the kids usually sat on the floor. Those two hours took us to America, to a country of tough guys that walked around Manhattan or Los Angeles, calling each other sons of bitches, while ordering coffee and asking strangers for the time. Also beautiful, white women, with big eyes and lips and breasts, in tight jeans. I thought everyone looked that way in America. My first encounter, however, occurred the day after I filled out my immigration forms, because the office was closed shortly after I was given the papers, the evening before. I handed in my forms to a different patient bureaucrat, and walked across the street to a donut and coffee shop, to practice my English on the cashier about to assist a fidgeting crowd of caffeine addicts on their way to work, behind me. A grotesquely obese woman with rollers in hair and scarring stretch-marks on the insides of her thighs below boxer shorts, stood in front of me. It was 9 in the morning. She ordered a dozen chocolate-glazed donuts and what looked like a three-liter coffee. Bless her poor heart. Imagine my surprise when I discovered the truth, that Americans are regular people with boring lives and fat, bitching women. I didn't understand why everyone was so upset. All I did was say, "I want a cup of coffee, son of a bitch," which I practiced for some time that morning. I didn't omit saying, "please" either. I found that I couldn't put hand on hand—where exactly it was that I missed the exit to civilization.

I would love to go back there someday. I've dreamt of it: A changed man, in a tailored suit; like a European. Rose-petals at my feat and begged to stay with some distant relatives. Walk in familiar streets, smell smells I have not held inside my breast for years. Talk to some childhood friends, if they are still alive. See what they are doing. The same thing as their fathers. Farming, selling, teaching children arithmetic. Who knows? Maybe one or two went into church. Became priests. Didn't know I was playing American cowboys and hide-and-seek with future alcoholics and prostitutes. Funny place, the world is. Probably bash my head against the wall, with Nostalgia, this feeling that makes you stand in place as though you are trapped in time, and you cannot move. The events most trivial at the time, become the most memorable. A ribbon is untied, and the present is a memory.

For this reason, I really don't despise my country. It's the people who made it the way it is. The rich exchange students in American universities, whose progenitors have made money on the enslavement of a population. Seeing their sons on the street isn't anything special. They are bulky, with ugly, human faces, as though their sculptor left them unfinished, or he was simply not a master of his craft. They drive expensive cars and go to exclusive clubs. They study economics and go to base-ball games. They fuck hot women. Or they're overworked students, molded as heirs to successful businesses that have managed to stash away a few unpleasant incidents on the road to their present condition. They live extravagantly, and you can't despise them as much as you can despise a dog for licking its balls. And you can't be disappointed in them for not being able to see the world for what it is. And you can't blame them for not being the ingenious sparks of reason, as so few people are in this world. I'm sure we all mean well, but have different ways of going about it. Now, I am beginning to understand what exactly it was that Fanon was trying to say. That violence, in its right, is the only way to change the world, because people do not change. People do not understand. So, I am taking my violence with me. This Friday night of violence, I will take my money, and I will leave, so help me God.

4

I was the highest ranking employee in charge that night. The police came to me first, although that Sunday morning was a closed book on the streets of every city.

Daphne Darling

1

I was fixing her jammed belt, hoping to get into her pants. Daphne was trying to explain something incommunicable to Sharon. They both wore nametags like retards, though only one of them had the misfortune. "I feel very lonely sometimes, you know?" she said from behind her long hair aglow like the city lights from last night.

"What honey?" Sharon asked.

"I said I feel lonely."

"Oh." Sharon's half-opened mouth, and head turned askew, with a look that dogs have, when they hear an odd, unfamiliar sound.

"I wish I had someone to talk to, someone to go to the movies with: You know, someone that *understands* me."

"You want to go to the movies with me?" Sharon was addled.

"Maybe."

"Do you want to go to the movies with me?" I took the opportunity

"That's sexual harassment."

"No it's not. It's two friends going out to the movies."

"Friends? I wouldn't say that."

"Sure, why not?"

"I don't even know your last name."

"I know yours."

"That's because I work here."

"Okay, it's Magezi-Akiiki."

"What the hell?"

I gave her a look.

"How do you pronounce it?"

With a hey and a ho, and a hey, nonnie, nonnie.

"Ma- ge-zi…"

"Ma- ge-zi," she repeated

"A- ki-i-ki."

"A- ki-i-ki. Say it again."

"Magezi-Akiiki."

"Magezi-Akiiki?"

"Yup."

"Where the hell's that from?"

"I'll tell you at the movies," I leaned in.

"Yeah, you wish." She turned away and didn't talk to me again for several minutes, until she started counting money. "You know, it's so tempting to just put all these bills in my pocket and go home."

"I wouldn't condone that."

"What's that?" Said the ghost of Sharon's intellect. I let her know she wasn't involved.

"Ha, I wish! Anyway, it wouldn't last me long." Thought Daphne.

"Well, that depends where you go."

"I don't know. Maybe hide somewhere? Live in Florida with my grandparents. My grandma would be like, 'Girl, where did you get all that money from?' and I'd be like, 'I won the lottery, grandma.' She'd be like, 'Praise the Lord!'"

"Or you could go to Africa, Asia, South America. The American dollar is worth more in certain countries."

"Hey thanks, boss! That's a great idea. But what would I do there? I don't speak nothing but English."

"You wouldn't need to, you'd have money. But it's probably a bad idea. Especially for you." I laughed.

"Why *especially* for me?"

"You'd get conned."

"No I wouldn't."

"Yes you would, as soon as you get there. You'd lose all your money to the taxi driver driving you from the airport."

"I'm not that stupid. Anyway, I'm just saying it's really unfair: Some people come here and spend what I make in a week. How can they do that?" she complained.

"Easy. They have good jobs.

"So, can I ask you something? What are you doing in the United States?"

I took the time to look at Daphne for a few moments so we both heard the resonance of her words amplify, "I live here," I said.

Her mistakes were reiterating thousands before. The basic questions: How do you say your name; how long have you been here; what are you doing here; where do you like it better. I'm tired of repeating the same thing over and over again. I'm from Uruguay. Where's that? South-East Asia. Really? Where do you like it better? I like it better there; people don't have to work as much. Why did you leave? Terrorists. My family, they perished. I'm sorry. That's alright; it was a long time ago. So what language do they speak there? Dutch. Really? I thought it was Spanish. Well, it used to be a colony of Belgium. Oh. *I acquired a sense of newfound respect in their eyes.* You speak very good English. Thank you.

But I didn't lie to Daphne.

2

Poor Daphne, she has to eat in the rank stench of processed food, spoiling dairy just three feet away from the public bathrooms, which service at least fifty people a day. The corner that is never cleansed builds strata of dirt lodging itself in the narrowest geometric crevice—the tip of a needle—like sponges that suck themselves up to the backs of whales and rocks. Little cancers, summoning their own blood vessels, growing sharp teeth to eat you faster. With each heave, she drags a piece to her delicate mouth, maintaining it behind her cheeks, tasting the salt which abets a floodgate of saliva. She swallows. She reads a book. I don't know if she sees the forty-yr-old retard with his mouth open staring at her. He doesn't blink. He has a large under-bite, and only one tooth. Even his last tooth is surrounded by a creeping, black annex starting from the root of the gums. A drool gravitates with IV-like opacity down his chin. He doesn't eat his lunch. He eats her. He chews. He swallows. Her. Another one, but a little younger, and with all teeth intact in a dark mouth, joins him. He's hungry, but still gives the calmly reading girl his full attention. It goes on like that for thirty minutes. She concentrates sternly. As though trying to set the book on fire. Something fantastical. Keeps her fingers very still. The clock hand is running in strange rhetorical arguments, never coming to conclusions. Forty-five minutes. She doesn't turn a single page.

I want to bash their brains in. I know what they're doing. They know what they're doing. That inexhaustible excuse of victimization behind the innocent, concerned, and duped physiognomies. Doesn't fool me, brother. No, sir. They can argue that their minds were stolen from them. They can't argue. I want to smash their heads against the wall like cantaloupes, when I see them look at Daphne that way. My poor Darling. She closes the book and packs away her lunch. One of them has the audacity to ask what she's reading. That fucker.

But I didn't proceed looking exceedingly at her tight, thin form; her delicate, sculptured neck, enhanced by the auspices of time, but undoubtedly indentured to them. "The Reading Girl," circa 1886—is how she had done that hair, color of the sun in window, and the face, the face it was red as snow. She lifted her head for a moment to look in the corner of a ceiling concentrating a point of thought that scatter spiders on the back wall, and illuminate. Soon I saw the drops born to the fruitful stuff of her head, and the two calf muscles of her eyelids, sobbing over the pages. Had I never seen it, I wouldn't have fallen in her hand dreamily holding a book.

3

"Do you think people will look at us funny?" she asked.

"Not if I introduce you as my daughter." I tried to hide the discomfort, far from humor. I had never been with anyone as young as she. Not that young! I'm not a pedophile. Ten year difference. Let them all look, eyes rolling off the table like cherries. She will wear something wool, like a young calf freshly shaved for summer. Legs pure and unmarked by time. And what of the waiter? A hot, flat iron bill should slap the look of his face.

"What do you think I should wear?"

"Something nice," I suggested

"What are you wearing?" She wouldn't stop.

"A suit," I said, "something nice too. You know, maybe it's not such a good idea to go. We don't have to go out. I mean, we could just stay here, order in some lobsters and a movie."

"No. We always do that." She was annoyed, "Of course I want to go! I'm tired of sitting around this place, and I can't get you to come home with me and you don't introduce me to your friends."

"I don't have too many friends."

"I want to go out. I want to do *something*."

"Ok, then. It's set." I watched her slip a dress on. "Come here before you go."

The mermaid slipped out of her scales, and the long hair still wet, hung longer to her back, covering her eyes that were open lids of oyster pearls. She looked younger. She came on command and lay down next to me. I admired her arm and shoulder blade praying upward, as she rested on her side. We lay together for 20 seconds.

"Now I don't want to go," she said.

4

I don't want an equal partner. I want to lead. I want control. Things are done more efficiently that way. Once you let her do any of the talking, she will think it's permissible to condescend all the time. You can't let women climb that pedestal. Otherwise, they'll chew you alive. And they do, I've seen it happen to my father. My mother chewed him out of the house, nagging. I have vivid memories of mornings waking up to the noise of running water and a large kettle boiling with bleach, bedsheets, and curtains. The birds spiraling outside to make their hoarse claims, the dog barking, god growling, children screaming from the playground; when the smoke of the bleach filled the room, and my mother's eyes were scalding red, she would begin the Sunday sermon, "You goddamn bastard, all you do is sit on your ass and drink. You never help me with anything. You're like a dog that needs to be trained. You don't take care of the children. They'll grow up hating you because you're fucking useless. Why do you keep spending my money? A normal man would try to support his children, but all you do is sit on your ass and drink" and so on and so forth. My father would stand in the bathroom, pissing and looking at me with the most pitiful eyes I have ever seen. She would fling a metal cup at him when she thought he wasn't listening. He would catch it, and reach under the kitchen table for the moonshine he got from the time she kicked him out of the house for talking to a young-girl neighbor. He left with his tail between his legs. So she began working on me; molding me to a sourpuss.

Daphne is not like that; she's young and impressionable.

When I look at Daphne, I can't imagine her aging. Sweet and shy as pie. Demure. She'll stay here the rest of her life. She will shrink and become old in her skin; the fragile hand of a child that tried to put on her mother's dress, unable to fill out its supple delicious curves.

Daphne was talking about something enthusiastically, with her shoulders bare. I couldn't concentrate because I was looking at a rather prominently plump zit on the acme of her shoulder blade. It had an annular ring of redness; cheesy it danced in her flesh, gyrating the terse layer—the leery top layer of dry skin that held it in place, like a cement dam with a slowly augmenting, thin crack in the monstrous thickness, not quite yet visible, she,

"Jennifer said that the only reason you're interested in me is because of sex."

"You told Jennifer? Jesus Christ, Daphne, that could get me fired." I, suddenly alert.

"Well, I didn't tell her about us. It was her who mentioned it. She said you were nice to anyone that was young and female and you do all the hiring since you're the manager."

"That's not true."

"Well, you're nice to me."

"I love you."

"I love you too. And I don't think it's true either. We have plenty of things in common."

"Yes we do." I said and switched the channel on TV.

Arthur Allan

Atlantic Drift

Dear Ellie:
    I want to tell you something that happened out here today. I hope you don't mind.

One moment it was bright as ever; the next, a massive slate cloud in front of the sun. Migrating birds, flying low. Thousands of them.

The wings pumped in synch, the uniforms of grey plumage passed in their great repeating pattern. The noise terrified me. A clamour of bullying squawks: keep going, don't pause, this is the way, this is what we do, this is the only direction.

When they had passed, one bird was left behind. It had taken refuge on the deck, exhausted. It wore a stunned, lopsided look as the din of the others faded.

For a while it shuffled gimpishly about. Then it stopped. Only its eyes twitched, aware that it was being watched. And people did glance at it as they passed, with disgust and embarrassment, hoping it would go away so they wouldn't have to deal with it.

It was gone when I went back above after supper. I suppose someone kicked it overboard.

My love (if I may),

Murray.

**** **** ****

Hello again Ellie,

More visitors today. A helicopter.

The clatter brought me out of my galley. Faces were twisted, hair blasted – except for the master, Desai, whose head preserved its neat matt outline. You could see people inside the chopper, one of them training a camera on us.

I edged onto an exposed patch of deck.

Desai flicked his arm, as if troubled by a mosquito. "Enough," he called. "What they expect, skull and crossbones?"

With a shrug, the helicopter turned away. I scurried back to my kitchen, my steaming pit.

It's the seventeenth day. As I work, moisture clogs my hair and beard. Run me through with a knife, Ellie – my juices would run clear. There are twenty-three men on board, and no place to eat: our cargo, unseen, claims the space. We squat on deck with our plates.

Twenty-four: I forgot myself.

"Something happened," Wolfe said in his grim sing-song.

He crouched by me on deck. The action squashed out the spare flesh of his legs below the shorts, bloating them.

"That news crew," he said. "They'd never chase us – "

"Uh-uh." I shook my head.

" – otherwise. It's way too late for them to be covering – "

"Uh-huh," I agreed.

" – the Turkey thing. I mean, what we're carrying,
they coulda been eco-freaks. Terrorists. But what do we
hear from Desai? Zip."

"Uh-huh." Wolfe is our navigator. To my surprise,
he has started to seek me out like this, sharing his out-
rage.

"But hey. You drown fifty-eight people, I guess this
is small beer." Wolfe shook his walnut head. "Later,
buddy."

I felt bolder after this exchange. Like I have the
same right as anyone else to walk this deck. Does that
seem strange to you?

Till tomorrow,

Murray.

* * * * * * * * * *

Ellie,

I'm sitting by the rail, squinting out at the sliver of
land that shines on the horizon. Currently, the Western
Sahara. It's the time when the sun is just about bearable, before it takes over the world and refuses to let us
look it in the eye. Another day. The helicopter already a
dream.

Desai himself has just wandered behind me, the
side of his mouth sucked into a crevasse. I need to
speak to him, but when I turned, he looked sideways. I
am fairly comfortable about this: I've learned that it's
not my presence that causes him to grimace and mutter,
or at least not me alone.

There's a story about most of the men, and even I

have absorbed them all. This is the story about Desai: he was master of a passenger ferry that went down off Mangalore, leaving many drowned. Despite an investigation that more or less absolved him, whispers persist about his culpability and the circumstances of his own survival amid the carnage.

I have no story. You know that, only too well. I've watched them mimic me – even the Indians and the Koreans – nodding their heads at each other with pneumatic vigour, in fervent assent, before breaking up in laughter. I haven't experienced such open contempt since school. Not that I blame them, Ellie. There's not much else to do out here.

Late last night, even in sleep, I detected some variation in the undernoise of our journey. The engines grinding in an unaccustomed way.

Disturbed, I switched on the lamp, conjuring up my coffin bunk. I picked up my book. But on this trip the words block up in front of my eyes. I'm trapped on the first page.

I started to wonder again if you would see the film taken by that camera. There would be no warmth in your thoughts, I know that. Still, I like the idea of you double-taking on a figure in a news bulletin, your nose furrowing as you recognise the slant of the shoulders, realise where I am. A connection of a kind.

Eventually the engines steadied, their sound slipping back below consciousness. My wee fantasy helped me sink under my seamy blanket and sleep.

Day eighteen. A precise rap on my door.

"Murray?" Wolfe's big domed cranium appeared. "Hey guy, you awake? Thought you'd wanna know. We've changed direction?"

It was phrased as an incredulous question. I folded

my bare arms away as he stooped to advance into the room.

"I mean ninety degrees. Seems like we're headed for Brazil, if you can believe it."

Fingernails clipped the ceiling as his big hands scooped disbelief from the air. There's a story about Wolfe too: it involves young girls.

"I wasn't on shift, I'm just off to find out what gives. Then again I'm only the fuckin' navigator, y'know?"

The practical implications came to me later, while I dumped breakfast onto plates. If we're not to land at Monrovia, we'll be forced onto dehydrated supplies within a couple of days. I will have to talk to Desai. If I marshal my words in my head, do my rehearsal first, it will be okay.

Wish me luck,

M.

**** **** ****

Hello Ellie.

Well, the master was in his mess with his back to the door. Praying, I thought. I hesitated, but he had caught my shadow, and he jerked his head to beckon me in.

He kept his hands cupped in front of him. Before I'd forced out a sentence he was nodding impatiently, eyes on the far wall. "I understand," he said. But I was locked into my dreary report and obliged to stutter through to its end. My face flamed, my torso was suddenly slick and reeking. You know the drill.

When he was sure I was done, Desai said, "Thank you, Murray." He opened his spidery hands, releasing two dice onto the tabletop. "I waiting instructions," he told the table. "Will be address the men this morning."

I slunk out. Desai dislikes formalities: I've seen him wince when addressed as sir or captain. It's not like the Royal Navy here, Ellie.

If I'm honest, the laxness isn't the main difference. Back then, I had the prospect of you to lace my days on board. I know you wouldn't want me to get sentimental, but if I do have a story – or at least a digression – it's you, Ellie. You know that.

I think of you in that Portsmouth office. Your couthiness, your bias for frilly collars. You didn't stand out for me at first. It was only gradually that I noticed how gravely and openly you looked at me in our exchanges – almost as though I was contributing something, other than instant confirmation. Not many people have your perseverance, faced with this unattractive, nodding, sweating little Scot. But when they do, eventually I relax enough in their presence to talk back, as I did with you. A remark about the wind, I think.

Sorry.

Desai assembled us on deck before lunch. He stood in the mouth of a horseshoe of men, smaller than any of us, like a kid run to ground by a posse. When he began to speak about a problem with the Liberian government, a tribal moan broke out.

"How long've you *known* this?" Wolfe whined, though quietly enough for Desai to ignore.

"Is difficult time." Desai paced a little, eyes darting out to the horizon. "I waiting instructions from the company."

Wolfe hissed in my ear, "Isn't *English* the international language of the sea?"

Helplessly, I nodded.

"I waiting instructions. You all hear news when I am hearing. Thank you for your patience. Meantime," Desai made a weak smile, "work to do." He ducked abruptly towards the bridge.

"Getting the finger from Turkey is one thing. But some banana republic?" Wolfe stabbed a thumb at the cargo hold, shouting now. "Is there something about this stuff we don't know? Is it unsafe or what?"

People murmured in similar tones, even as they drifted aside. I've noticed how men wriggle out of Wolfe's radius. I always used to think that was unfair. But in my bunk this morning, feeling the heat of his frustration, his spittle on my cheek – I got a glimpse of how those little girls might have felt. If they ever existed.

Goodnight now,

M.

**** **** ****

Ellie,

I could do with your opinion about something that happened last night.

I was pacing the deck, swaddled in layers. The nights are cold enough to strip your face. I stopped at the barrier to the hold. No one goes beyond this, except the men kitted out with boxy suits and masks. I've sometimes wondered what it looks like, the material we're carrying. I imagine it as a pale, cheese-like substance. I see it in casks the size of swimming-pools, gently fluorescent in the shadows, steaming slightly. I'd like to scramble onto that yielding surface and lie there on my back, adjusting to the heat. Sinking, gradually, into its humid mass. Merging with the unwanted gunk of the world.

Somebody sniffed behind me. I knew who it was before I turned. I confess: I've been relishing Wolfe's pursuit of me and what it seems to mean. His singling out my door to rap on. "Guy." "Buddy."

He used it now: "Restless, buddy?"

"Uh-huh."

"You're not the only one. Things're set to blow around here." He leaned on the barrier alongside me, thrusting out a slender bottle. "Beat the chill."

I tipped it and whisky beetled deep into my gullet, hot and electric.

"Alcohol gets a bad rap, man. Sometimes it's the only way out. When you got no control over where you're heading."

Take my agreement as read.

"I mean, I'm not ashamed to say I been bruised. I'd guess you have too. I guess we all have, otherwise why'd we be out on this floatin' junkyard? Yeah, I hit a real low a couple years ago."

Struck by the sight of our elbows paired on the rail, I took a while to realise what he was telling me. His story.

There were three girls. Wolfe said he didn't touch them. He had no interest in doing so. He never told me their ages (I didn't ask). When one girl learned about the other two, Wolfe said, she got jealous and told her mother. Wolfe spent three months in jail.

"You wanna know the fuckin' irony? My PC was shot. I never even uploaded them pictures. Never enjoyed the fruits of my *evil crime*. Hell, Jody? – the one who told her mom? – she actually begged me to take more. Wanted to take them to an agency." His meaty hand thumped down on my arm. "It's a bitch, fella. Go through something like that, it marks you every hour of the day and night."

I said – well, you know what I said. But for once I wasn't agreeing purely out of compulsion. There was a sweet sharpness in my throat. My vision was bubbling up. What he said was nearly irrelevant. It was the sight of his words spilled for me, the gracefully-tumbling clouds they formed between us on the night air.

It was only afterwards, scrubbing in the shower, that I started to wonder.

I don't expect a reply from you. I just thought setting it down might shed a new light, show me what your take on this would be.

But I suppose you're too far away for that now.
M.

**** **** ****

Ellie.

The twentieth day was like all the others, but more so. The sun pressed down more heavily, glared more insistently in my eyes. As we followed our tight, rat-like circuits – above, below, above again – the air held a sourer tang of sweat, a greater density of cursing than normal. A few little flares of pointless shout and shove. The food I nervously served up was greyer, visibly reconstituted rather than cooked.

"We could take over the radio," Wolfe said when I approached him. "Let the company know Desai's brain is fried."

I said, quite smoothly I think, "Actually, it's the company I blame. They're well-known to be cowboys. I think probably they're in over their heads, don't know what to do next."

When I managed to raise my eyes from the deck Wolfe was gaping at me, his face twisted with incomprehension. It was as if he'd been addressed by a seagull.

Eventually he said, "You're – what? Irish?"

I grinned shyly. "I'm a S-scot." The word leaked out in a slow puncture.

"No kidding. I always thought you were American." He shook his head briskly. "I mean, guys are freaking here and he's just not around. What does he do all day, anyhow?"

"Games."

"Huh?" His incredulity grew.

"He throws – he throws dice sometimes. I saw him in his mess. But W-wolfe, I really think he's as screwed as we are in this."

Wolfe flinched at the sound of his name. He looked at me hard. "You...think. You think, huh? Dice," he muttered to himself. "We're in crisis, and Desai's playing fuckin' Monopoly." And he barrelled past me.

Now it's the twentieth night, and my body's too cold for sleep, and my mind is too tattered to read.

M.

**** **** **** ****

Well, Ellie,

It's over.

As we awaited the master's arrival, I sought out Wolfe. By now, his likely location was constantly fixed on my personal radar, but I'd not seen him since yesterday. I found him at the rail, in conversation with Lee, a stocky Korean.

"Does he even keep a log? If he does, nobody's seen it," Wolfe was ranting. "You gotta keep some kind of record. That's maritime law."

I hovered, sipping water.

"A master needs communication skills. He comes to me this morning, he says, 'North'. I say, what, you wanna change course, is there a reason, where are we headed? Just that. 'North.' And he's already walking away!"

Wolfe barked his incredulous laugh. I saw Lee, who has virtually no English, smile obligingly.

"What I'm gonna do is contact the TV news. They can get that helicopter back here and chart where we've been the last few days. *That*'d be one helluva story."

I pushed myself off the rail, making for the gap between the men. But Wolfe raised his hand abruptly to clap Lee's shoulder, closing up the angle of their bodies.

"I dunno about you, buddy," he said, "but I'm going crazy here. One thing I can't take, it's losing control over my life. Did I tell you what happened to me a couple years ago?"

It was a smooth movement, my swerve, as though it had been my intention all along to walk towards the bridge. And it will be an equally seamless shift back to my old existence. A friendship, especially one this unripe, is easily killed, Ellie. It's not like a marriage. There's been no long build-up of suppressed contempt and revulsion. I didn't oblige him to spend years prising me off.

I went to warn Desai. Probably Wolfe was all talk, but if he were to compromise us in the way he'd said, that would be a disciplinary issue. The old navy training resurfacing in me. Anyway, I no longer had to consider any loyalty to Wolfe.

But the master's mess was empty. When I got back, he was already on deck, starting his speech. And the murmurs were rising. The gist – actually, the full message – was that negotiations were ongoing. Meantime, we wait.

"The company, they working on it," Desai was saying.

"The fuck they are!" Wolfe burst forward, loomed above Desai, cords standing out on his slick forehead. "How long you gonna keep us going round in circles out here? How long you gonna keep feeding us this shit, huh?"

The men watched thirstily. For a moment the pair were frozen there: Wolfe with his great fists bunched; Desai, short and fine, his eyes lost under the bigger man's shadow.

Then the master calmly moved his hands behind his back. A gesture that said: Do it. Hit me. "The company working on it," he repeated, in the same flat tone.

It was his utter disinterest that restored his authority, and I sensed every man on deck realise that Wolfe's anger is wasted effort. There won't be a coup against Desai. Where would Wolfe take us, given command? Going nowhere is our duty. What we're carrying is leprous. No one knows what to do with it. Nobody cares where it ends up, so long as it's not on their territory.

Held air was released, Wolfe sank back in frustration. Desai's eyes flicked lightly round the semi-circle, settling on a point in mid-ocean. And me, I felt my spirits begin to lift, float free.

I've been wrong about Desai. What I took for timidity – it was pure detachment. The man we see here is just a hollow device, tethered and bobbing on the surface; the real Desai is sunk at some dark, fathomless point, miles away.

If you did by some chance spot me in that news film, Ellie, forget it. And you'll be pleased to hear, I won't be writing to you any more – not even like this, forming the letters with my tongue, on the roof of my mouth. Take this as goodbye.

I've spent so long straining, following instincts that were always redundant for me anyway – tormenting myself, exhausting myself. When all I needed to do was emulate Desai. Embrace the routine of drift.

Day twenty-one, and this is where I stop counting.

His mess had been empty, when I went to warn him. I entered anyway, reluctant to waste my rehearsed words, and stood in the sparsely furnished room, tidy to the point of blankness. On the scarred pine table, in diagonally opposite corners, lay the solitary mark of personalisation – those two dice. I noticed felt-tip scrawling alongside the spots, and bent to look closer. On one side, I made out the letter S; another bore a W. And on the upward face of each cube, the neat slant of an N.

Notes on Contributors

Arthur Allan is an Edinburgh-based freelance journalist. *Atlantic Drift* is his third published story. Inevitably (he says) he's working on a novel, provisionally titled *Nine Monsters*.

Jonathan Attrill writes both fiction and poetry. His work has been published in a variety of literary magazines and anthologies. In 2004 he won the London Writers' Competition with his short story "Darker Than Fairytales". He is a regular reader at venues across London, including *Tales of the Decongested's* monthly short story readings at Foyles. He facilitates a creative writing class in North London for people with mental health problems.

Shakti Bhatt is an editor based in New Delhi. She is working on her first novel.

Willie Davis is a native of Whitesburg, Kentucky who currently teaches English at The University of Maryland. "Kid in a Well" (winner of the Willesden prize) is a chapter from *The Darktown Strut*, his recently completed novel about contemporary Appalachian life.

Steve Finbow is from London. He used to live in New York. He now resides in Japan. A long time, ago he worked for Allen Ginsberg. He once assisted Richard Long. He even did research for Victor Bockris and Barry Miles. Nowadays, he sits around reading and writing. The Guardian, The Independent, McSweeney's, Stop Smiling, Me Three, and a host of other publications have published his work. Some of his short stories have appeared in anthologies. Some have not. He is an occasional writer with Quarantine Theatre Company. He is a diabetic "but not a very good one" and so "enjoys hospital food and the works of Elmore Leonard, James Kelman, and Martin Amis." His favourite journey is riding Tokyo's Yamanote Line loop. His biography "reads better than it lives." For more information, go to: www.seppukumyheart.blogspot.com.

Vanessa Gebbie left behind a career in journalism to focus on creative writing in 2003. Since then her short fiction has been widely published. She's had success in competitions, "the crown of which," (she says!), "was a win at Willesden in 2006". Other wins include BBC Guildford Book Festival competition, Charleston Small Wonder Festival Slam, Cadenza Magazine, The Phoenix Prize 2006, Cotswold Writers, JBWriters Bureau. Her stories have been short-listed three times at Fish International, long-listed for the Bridport Prize, commended at Writers of the Year and Winchester, broadcast by the BBC, read at performance events, and distributed on London Underground in *Litro*. Vanessa adds that she is working on a novel "but they all say that!" She also teaches Creative Writing to marginalised adults. For more information please visit: www.vanessagebbie.com.

Nicholas Hogg was born in Leicester in 1974. After travelling widely, living in Japan, Fiji and America, he is now settled in London teaching literary skills to refugees. Winner of the inaugural New Writing Ventures prize for fiction, and twice short-listed for the Eric Gregory award, he has recently completed his first novel, *Show Me the Sky*. Online: www.nicholashogg.com

Laura Heggie was born in Devon in 1982. She is a graduate of the University of East Anglia Creative Writing MA course, and lives in North West London. She is working on her first novel, about punishment and beauty in mid-20th century France. "*Avoiding the Issue* was inspired by a Big Issue seller in Bath, who told me to buy a Big Issue from him, then carry it around visibly under my arm, so other homeless people wouldn't ask me for money."

Lee Joans is an English-born writer. In her twenties she worked as a nurse and clinical editor. Recently she completed her first novel and she is planning to read for a PhD in literature. *Vaselino* is adapted from a novel-in-progress. Contact: LeeJoans@hotmail.co.uk

James Lawless was born in Dublin and lives in Kildare. He is an arts graduate of UCD and has an MA from Dublin City University. Recently he took early retirement from teaching to concentrate on writing full time. He has had stories and poems broadcast on radio and published in journals and anthologies in Ireland and England. He won the Scintilla Welsh open poetry competition in 2002, and the Cecil Day Lewis play section award in 2005 for a play entitled, "What are Neighbours For?" At the moment he is working on a novel.

Wes Lee is originally from the UK and currently living in New Zealand. A former printmaker & University Lecturer in Fine Arts, she now works in an art gallery and writes. In 2006 she was awarded First Prize in the City of Derby Short Story Competition and Runner-up in the Writers of the Year Award; the Biscuit Publishing Prize and the Australasian short story competition "Auswrite". She was a finalist in the Guildford Book Festival/BBC Southern Counties Radio Short Story Competition and the Cadenza Short Story Prize. Her writing has appeared in numerous online and print publications, including: Cadenza, Buzzwords, Opium Magazine, PopMatters, The HazMat Review, Turbine, Trout, Takahe, VerbSap, Snorkel, The Ugly Tree, The BluePrint Review, Blowback Magazine, Misanthropists Anonymous, Mannequin Envy, HeavyGlow, On New Street: Biscuit International Prize-winning Short Stories, The Final Theory & Other Stories, Survival Guides, All Over The Place: Writers of the Year Anthology, The Weather Man: Best of the Skive Short Story Prize. She has work forthcoming in a number of anthologies in the UK.

Olesya Mishechkina is a Perestroyka baby immigrant, hopping from Alaska to Arizona, finally settling in the leafy state of Massachusetts. "Blowing off a free college education after two full years, in hopes of becoming a writer, I found myself 19, working as a grocery store cashier, and sleeping on my mother's couch. If that's not idealism, I don't know what is."

Laura Solomon was born in New Zealand in 1974, and has lived in London since 1999. She has an honours degree in English Literature (Victoria University,

NZ, 1997) and a Masters degree in Computer Science (University of London, 2003) and currently works as an IT consultant. She has published two novels in New Zealand with Tandem Press: "Black Light" (1996) and "Nothing Lasting" (1997). Her first play, "The Dummy Bride", was produced as part of the Wellington Fringe Festival, and her second, based on her short story, "Sprout", was part of the 2004 Edinburgh Fringe Festival. Her short story "Sprout" won a prize in the 2004 Bridport International Short Story competition and her short story "The Most Ordinary Man in the World" won a prize in the same competition in 2005. She has published various other poems and short stories online and in New Zealand magazines.

www.ingramcontent.com/pod-product-compliance
Lightning Source LLC
Chambersburg PA
CBHW050508260626
47157CB00004B/1241